This is a people, places,
THE FAT

Second edition. March, 2023.
Copyright © 2023 Carla Rossi.
Written by Carla Rossi.

THE FATHER-DAUGHTER PICNIC

Carla Rossi

Welcome to Cardinal Point, Texas.

Where the broken find comfort,
the prodigals find peace,
and the wanderers find home.
And... you just might see a cardinal.

Bachelor #1 - Disappointing Davey and the Disastrous Dinner Date

Caroline Bishop maneuvered her napkin to hide the splash of vinaigrette on her pink silk blouse. If her date noticed, he was doing a good job of averting his eyes from the wet outline of Germany now spreading on her chest.

She gave up the charade of being a confident non-klutz and let the napkin fall to her lap. "I think it's obvious I dropped an oil-soaked piece of lettuce on my blouse. I'm not proud, but there's nothing I can do about it this minute."

Davey leaned in, made eye contact, and did everything a polite man would do on a date to engage a potential girlfriend and set her at ease. "Hardly noticeable," he said with a smile, and it seemed he would have touched her arm or patted her hand if they knew each other any better.

Kind. He was kind. And attentive. That earned him solid consideration for a second date. He was cute, too, even with the two distracting stray hairs that kept trying to abandon his right eyebrow. Thicker than the rest of his hair and wiry, they sprang to attention as if trying to escape across his forehead. Did he not feel them up there? It took monumental restraint to not lick her thumb and smooth them into place.

Note to self: if there's a second date, bring tweezers.

"Did you get caught in the rain?" he asked.

"No. Made it in the nick of time."

He smiled. "Seems March wants to go out like a lion."

She picked up her water glass. "Well, here's to April having more sunshine."

He toyed with a beverage napkin and traced the outline of the restaurant's logo, a stylized bird on a branch with their name. "I've never been here. I don't get out of Austin much, but I like Cardinal Point, and this place has great reviews."

She swept a mass of dark hair off her shoulder. "I'm not surprised. It's the most authentic Italian you can get in this part of Texas."

He held up the napkin. "You're a local. How do you say this?"

"*Uccello Rosso.*"

He tried. And failed. And laughed about it. "Sorry. Language is not my strong suit. What does it mean?"

"Quite literally, Red Bird."

"Ah. Because we're in Cardinal Point. Do you speak Italian?"

"Only enough to be dangerous. Right now, I have an app on my phone that lets me capture characters and phrases and it translates them for me. I'd like to learn a lot of languages, but I stay busy at work and with my daughter, so there's not much extra time."

He didn't flinch at the mention of a daughter. She'd made it clear in her online dating profile she came as a package deal. Still, men couldn't generally hide their misgivings about taking on someone else's kid. The remark hadn't fazed him. Another positive sign.

He pushed away his salad plate. "Tell me about your work at the nursing home."

Caroline pinched her own thigh under the table to keep from snapping back. She hated the words *nursing home*. Might as well call it a *rest home* or a *convalescent center* or an *old folks' home*. People had been calling it those names forever and most of them didn't know the difference, but her patients fought tooth and nail in rehab to be able to resume normal activities. Many were young victims of a failing body or devastating accidents. As for the others, they weren't *convalescing*. They were likely terminal, and trying to maintain some dignity until the end. It was her job to make sure they all got what they needed—especially when family was scarce or worse, neglectful.

She set her fork across her plate. "It's not really a nursing home. We have two sections. There's in-patient rehabilitation for people who've had a stroke or injury and need various therapies to recover and safely return to their homes. The other branch is a skilled nursing facility. Those patients require long-term care and may or may not be able to improve with therapy or return home."

"But you're not a doctor?"

"No. I'm a hospital administrator. But I work with all the doctors who are in charge of various aspects of patient care."

"My mother was in a nursing home," he said as he squeezed the stem of his water goblet. "She was there until she passed. It was a bad experience."

Once again, she pinched her thigh. If he was going to tell her some horror story about bed sores or elder abuse... "I'm sorry to hear that." She really was sorry to hear that, and she'd want to know more someday. But not over first date manicotti.

"They didn't respect any of our wishes with medication. We wanted all genetic medication, and they kept insisting it wasn't always available."

Genetic medication?

Curiosity got the best of her, and no amount of thigh-pinching was going to keep her from diving in. "I'm not following. What do you mean by genetic medication? Were you trying to get approval for non-approved new drugs or something?"

"No, genetic drugs. The fake drugs. You know, the knock-offs of the expensive name-brands."

"Oohhh... you mean *generic* drugs," she said and then wished she hadn't so pointedly corrected him.

"Yes. That's what I said. Genetic."

Pinch, pinch, pinch...

He said language wasn't his strong suit. Apparently, English was too much for him too.

There would be no second date with this one. No lingering over coffee and dessert, and no future plans. She'd only barely convinced herself there might be. Truth was, she knew from the handshake in front of the restaurant it would go nowhere. Zero chemistry, zero attraction, zero desire to find out more.

Oh. And he wasn't her late husband Jason, so he'd started the evening already two strikes behind in the count. If not for her daughter Ava, she wouldn't be here at all.

*Ava...*The only reason she was at Cardinal Point's best restaurant with a stranger on a Thursday night, and the only reason she would power through and make the best of it until a suitable match came along.

THE FATHER-DAUGHTER PICNIC

Their server arrived with steaming plates as a rumble of hearty male laughter floated from a nearby private dining room.

"We apologize," the waitress said as she waved a cheese grater. "They get loud sometimes."

"Who are *they*?" Caroline asked, though she didn't mind, didn't care who they were, and wasn't interested in why they were loud. She sought only to have a longer conversation with her waitress than she did her date.

"Chamber of Commerce people. They have standing meetings here a couple times a month. Sometimes more. Can I get you anything else right now?"

"No. Thank you."

Another boom of laughter distracted Davey mid-sentence, and Caroline let her fork stick in the melting cheese when she saw a certain man leave the loud room with his phone.

No, no, *no*.

Not Graham Hollister.

Not tonight.

The sharp-dressed man buttoned his well-tailored suit jacket with one smooth move of his hand. His smile never left his face as he walked across the room with too much swagger and probably way too much cologne.

He winked at the hostess.

That might've made Caroline gag, but he sat so low on her list of people deserving a response, she didn't bother.

From what she'd seen, Graham Hollister was all about business and money, and nothing about loyalty and family.

Nothing.

She grabbed a knife and sliced away at the gooey, ricotta-filled pasta on her plate. *Please, please, please don't let him see me...*

"Ms. Bishop. I thought that was you."

She looked to the ceiling. *Wow. First Disappointing Davey and now Gut-Grating Graham.*

She forced a smile and held her napkin to hide the stain. "Mr. Hollister. Pleasure to see you."

Davey tried to do the gentlemanly thing and stand.

Graham waved him off. "No, don't get up. Don't want to disturb you."

But they did do the obligatory business-y male introduction thing where Graham said his name loud enough that the surrounding diners would hear the mighty voice of the new banker in town and be duly impressed.

"Well," he said and turned his oozing charm on her. "I'll get out of your way." His wildflower blue eyes locked with hers then travelled to the napkin clutched at her chest. The trip back up was far too slow. "*Buono cena.*"

"*Grazie.*" The word fell out of her mouth with a perfectly rolled *r* and way too much appreciation for an arrogant boob like Graham Hollister. Especially since she was only moderately sure *buono cena* meant *have a good dinner...* or something like that.

Wait a minute.

Graham Hollister did *not* get to commit a drive-by flirting. He didn't get to interrupt her date and cast some voodoo smolder her way with his pretty blue eyes.

He didn't get to make her speak Italian.

"Mr. Hollister?"

He turned. "Yes?"

"How is your father today? I didn't get by to see him. Have you seen him? At all?"

A sour expression chased the confident smile and teasing smirk right off his face. "I'm sure he's doing well in your facility's care. I didn't see him today. Maybe tomorrow."

"Maybe tomorrow," she repeated. "There's always tomorrow."

"Club soda," he said.

"Excuse me?"

"Club soda." He pointed at her chest. "Works every time."

CAROLINE KICKED OFF her shoes in the garage and padded toward the kitchen in hopes of not running into anyone. And by anyone, she meant Bette, her late mother's totally awesome and irreplaceable friend who lived with her and Ava and took care of them since Jason's death. Truly, Caroline couldn't have made it without her—even though she could live without her habit of leaving tea bags, tea cups, and half-used sweetener packets all over the house. Seriously, did the woman ever actually drink the numerous cups of tea she poured?

"This is quite possibly the lamest Walk of Shame I have ever witnessed." Bathed in light from the pendant over the sink, Bette sat at the kitchen table in her fuzzy socks and candy-heart green chenille robe. "It's... It's... devastatingly sad."

Caroline dropped her purse on the table. "It's eight-thirty, Bette. This is not a Walk of Shame. Not even close. In fact, I'm so far from a Walk of Shame I can't even see it from here. And I'm a good girl, remember? None of that for me."

"How was the food?"

"Food was great, but I had to pinch my thigh like seven times."

"You've got to break that habit. You have a permanent bruise there and it's almost swimsuit season. You're going to give yourself a blood clot or spider veins or, at the very least, a whopper of a varicose vein. It's painful to have those bad boys fixed."

"That's the least of my worries."

"Might as well tell me all of it," Bette said as she dangled a tea bag over her steaming mug. "Can I get you a cup of herbal?"

"No, thanks. I need to check on Ava."

"She's out for the night. C'mon, sit down."

Caroline untucked her blouse from her charcoal gray pencil skirt. "He insisted I call him Davey. Not David, not Dave, but *Davey*. I felt like a pre-school teacher all night. *How's your salad, Davey? Did you have a nice drive from Austin, Davey? I hope you didn't have to park your tricycle too far from the restaurant, Davey.* Is it me, or is that weird? What grown man in business wants to be called *Davey*?"

Bette started a slow shrug and a massive over-the-top eye roll. "Nooooo," she said, low and breathy, as if horrified. Her hazel eyes twinkled in the dim light. "You mean he wasn't *the one*? I can't believe it. He looked so perfect on your iPad."

"Don't. Start. I know you're not on board with my plan, but it has to be done."

"No, it doesn't, Caroline. You can't manufacture what you're trying to manufacture here. You can't order a new father for Ava online and wait for UPS to drop him off at your door."

"Why is that, Bette? Why can't it be that simple? I can find everything else online. Why not a dad for Ava?"

Bette tucked a lock of *sunshine blonde #47* behind her ear and leaned in to squeeze Caroline's hand. "Oh, honey, I know you're lonely. It's been close to two years since Jason, but it has to happen naturally."

"It's not about me. I'm not lonely. I'm... hollow. It's Ava. She can't grow up like I did with an absent father. Everything was lopsided. I didn't learn the things girls are supposed to learn about men because there was never a man in our house. My mother didn't date. She didn't even try. No wonder I went looking for that fatherly influence in all the wro—"

"Stop it, Caroline. Stop it right now. You're obsessing again. A second ago we were discussing preschooler Davey. Now we're on your rebellious teen years and your crackpot mother? Believe me, I loved that woman. She was my best friend, but she was nuts. It was hard for you, but we've been through all this. Stop it."

Caroline gripped the edge of the table until her pastel-colored spring tablecloth pulled away from the edges and bunched under her fingertips. She always did this. She spiraled and went back in time and entertained long-forgiven and long-forgotten sins. She dredged up past hurts and resurrected ancient crimes against herself.

Quickly, she took captive her own thoughts. One by one, she stacked them in her head like multi-colored blocks and knocked them down and swept them away. *Focus. Focus on Ava.*

Focus on the future. "You're right. I know you're right. I'm done with all that."

"Listen, honey, you were dealt a really bad hand, but you made it. You grew up and made something of yourself. You found a great man who loved you and brought a beautiful child into this world. You lost a lot when you lost Jason but, once again, you came out the other side and you're moving forward."

"Then why do you have such a problem with my master plan to find a father for Ava?"

"Because you can't conjure up what you and Ave really need by filling out a questionnaire. You're not using your heart, or chemistry, or your femininity to attract a man. You're using logic. There's no room for logic in a love affair."

"I'm not looking for a love affair like I had with Jason. I already experienced the love of my life and he's gone. I don't expect weak knees and passion. I want stability, companionship, and a two-parent home for Ava."

"*Ppppffffttttt! Pleeease.* Don't forget that men aren't always what they present themselves to be. Having a man around isn't the answer to everything and can go bad pretty quick. You know that. You're a smart capable woman in your own right. Don't forget that."

"I know all that."

"OK, then. Can't you do what I said earlier and let this happen naturally? Let love find you. Let it sneak up on you and surprise you."

"You sound like a jewelry store commercial during Valentine season." Caroline turned her head to each side to loosen her muscles and ward off a tension headache. "Time is running out. Ava is six. She needs the influence of a decent man now."

"What do you think a man can do around here that we can't? I mean besides the blissfully obvious things he could do to keep that knot of tension away." Bette winked and wiggled her eyebrows like some tipsy bachelorette at a male strip club.

Caroline strangled a laugh before it got out. No use encouraging the woman. "Knock it off, you man-crazy maniac."

"Watch it. I'm no maniac. I like to get taken to dinner and the movies. I like waiting for it to happen naturally." She pulled a pair of lavender readers and a piece of notebook paper from her robe pocket. "Anyway, while I think your plan to land a husband—excuse me, a *father* for Ava, which I still don't see how you think you can separate the two—is a harebrained scheme at best, I do know it's not possible to drive a parked car. You have to start the thing and drive it once in a while to find the right road. With that in mind, I started a list of eligible men in Cardinal Point. If you really want a mate, you should put on your high heels and your push-up bra and see who comes a-runnin.'"

"I am not a prostitute."

Bette set her glasses on her nose. "True, true, but you're not a nun either. Men are visual. You know this. They fall in love with who they're attracted to. That starts with the presentation."

"I'm going to bed."

"First on the list: Cole Boudreaux. Now *that's* a man."

"Nope. Most assuredly off the market. I met him at the Mistletoe Gala back in December. He runs that B&B with the gymnastics coach from the rec center."

"You think it's solid?"

Caroline shot her an *I can't believe you said that* glare and started to stand again.

"OK, OK, never mind. Sit back down. Next up: Shane Calfee."

"What is he, like *twenty*? He's too young for me. Cute as a bachelor button, I guess, but all that boy-next-door blond hair and blue eyes... No. Not my type."

"All right, then. How about dark hair and dark blue eyes? As in Graham Hollister. New guy who runs the bank."

Caroline snorted. "Ummm.... *No*. Big fat negative on that one."

"Why? He's so sweet."

"He is not sweet. He's....obnoxious, arrogant, self-centered..." Caroline waved her hands to keep the flow coming. "... pompous, pretentious, shallow..."

Bette peeked over the top of her glasses. "Are you finished? All those words mean the same thing."

"No, they don't. They each have a different slant." Caroline raised her hands as if to shove the whole idea away from her. "Doesn't matter anyway. I'm not interested in Graham Hollister."

Bette sat back in the chair and tapped pink fingernails against her ceramic mug. "This is amusing."

"What?"

"Me thinks the lady doth protest too much."

"The man's a jerk, Bette, I don't want him."

"He's only been here a few months. How could you already like him so little?"

"The better question is, how you could you like him so much?"

The older woman dropped her gaze and traced the petite yellow flowers on the cloth. "He helped me the other day."

"What did you do, Bette?"

"My debit card may have been stolen. OK, not stolen. I may have lost my debit card. OK, not lost, so much as left it at the craft store counter and forgot about it for days. Someone may have racked up some charges to my account. I had to go to the bank and sort it out, and Graham was very helpful when me and Ava went by there after school."

"You subjected my innocent baby to Graham Hollister?"

Bette laughed out loud. "He's not a monster, Caroline. He was great with her."

"Does this debit card story have a happy ending? I'm tired, and now I'm worried about you."

"Don't be ridiculous. When I got to the bank, I told the girl what had happened. Graham was standing there when she called me Betty. You know how I hate that. Graham picked up my paperwork and said *I'm guessing she pronounces her name Bette. Like Bette Midler.* Then he remarked on my obvious resemblance to *The Divine Miss M*." Bette fluffed her hair and struck a pose. "I still got it. Then we went to his office and he gave Ava a juice box and got her a bag of popcorn from the popper in the lobby. He fixed everything and gave me a new card, and he and Ava talked about horses."

"Horses?"

"Yes, you know she's all about those toy ponies with the long manes and the glitter. Graham has horse stuff all over his office. I guess his family has a lot of them. He said they board horses for other people. He said the person who runs his barn gives lessons and all that. We should sign Ava up."

"No."

"Why not? She's had a fascination with horses forever. It would teach her responsibility and all that."

"Horses can be dangerous. She's tiny. They're huge."

"Stop it, Caroline. They put kids in helmets and pads to take the trash out these days. I'm sure she'd be fine."

"Is your debit card issue resolved and the stolen money back in your account? Is there any chance the other cards you carry were compromised? Like the one you have from my account?"

"Everything's fine. I wouldn't have bothered you with it if I hadn't stumbled on that gem of a guy Graham Hollister."

Caroline clutched the sides of her head and squeezed. "He's not a gem of a... you know what? Never mind. I'm tired. We'll *not* talk about this tomorrow. I'm going to go watch my daughter sleep for a while and then get to bed."

"Suit yourself. Toss me that blouse."

"Why?"

"Stain. Club soda."

"I know. I'll do it."

"No. Toss it over. I'll do it."

Caroline shed the blouse. "Thanks."

"Anything for you, my love." Bette studied the stain. "What do you really have against Graham Hollister?"

"You can tell a lot about a person by the way they treat their parents." Caroline lifted her purse from the table. "Graham Hollister is not a good son."

Candidate #1 - The Backward Banker

Graham Hollister welcomed Jim Hunt's boy—Jim, Jr.—into his office and motioned to a leather wingback chair. "Good to see you, Jim."

Jim sat and placed his folder in his lap. He moved in that awkward way he did when the Hollister and Hunt boys all played ball together and ran wild on each other's property. "Everyone still calls me J.R.," he said and smiled.

J.R. was only about six years younger, but he seemed to be such a boy. He dressed the grown-up part and Graham knew he was nearing the end of a business and finance degree at the University of Texas, but J.R. Hunt didn't come off as a serious candidate for a managerial position at Hollister & Sons National Bank.

Graham glanced at his resume and then placed it face down on his desk. A person could put anything on the page. That didn't mean a thing, and now Graham felt obligated to share life and business experience with the tenderfoot. God knew, he'd learned everything the brutally hard way—and was still being schooled by a team of federal investigators in Houston who could either pull him out from under a cloud of suspicion, or drown him in its downpour.

"I'll call you J.R. because we're old friends, but you might want to ditch that nickname outside of Cardinal Point."

Graham hadn't seen anyone so confused since he asked his dad's assistant for the name of the bank's cyber security consultant. *That* had turned into the longest day he experienced since his return to Cardinal Point.

"Here's the thing," Graham continued. "You're a real Texas cowboy, raised on your father's ranch. The original *Dallas* hasn't been on since the eighties, but everyone still seems to know something about J.R. Ewing. You ride into an interview in New York City's financial district and you won't be taken seriously. You're Jim Hunt. That's who you are. You're not a Texas stereotype with boots and a hat."

The kid looked uncomfortable, but seemed to get it. "Point taken. My relatives in Pennsylvania think we all have derricks in our back yards."

Graham eased back in his chair. "Now, why are you here today?"

Once again, confusion ruled the moment. "Uh... My father sent me."

Graham figured as much. The senior Jim Hunt had been dogging him about J.R. since he got back in town. Just another over-reaching parent trying to nail down their son's future with no regard for what the son might want or be qualified for.

Graham snatched the resume off the desk because J.R. sure wasn't going to share anything, and appeared to lack the confidence to declare white or wheat when he ordered a sandwich at Songbird's Bakery and Café.

"This is a fine resume. You've joined all the right organizations, earned all the right recognition, taken all the right career steps. The only thing you haven't done is tell me you want a job at my dad's bank. Do you, J.R.? Do you want a job at this bank when you get out of school in May?"

J.R. went from pale to pink and splotchy. The tips of his ears burned red beneath the smooth line of his fresh-from-the-barber haircut. The kid didn't want to work at the bank any more than he wanted a free, roadside colonoscopy.

Graham scooted his chair back. "I'm going to make this easy for you. You trust me, right? Because we're old friends?"

J.R. nodded.

"All right, then, I'm going to take the pressure off this meeting." Graham fed the resume through the paper shredder under his desk. "Don't worry," he said when J.R. looked like he'd lose the donut and coffee he saw him snag from the lobby, "I'll take care of this with your dad. I'll tell him you followed through, but it wasn't a good fit at this time. This one's on me."

"Sure, Graham."

"The truth is, J.R., you really aren't a good fit for us at this time. With my dad's riding accident and the head injury, I don't know how long he'll be away or if he'll ever come back to manage the bank. He'd mentioned retirement, but no one believed him. He may not have a choice now. I have a career in Houston I have to get back to. I have to leave the bank in the hands of someone with experience. The new board is taking us in a different direction. Cardinal Point is growing. We're going to put a satellite branch in the grocery store out by the freeway, and we'll need a new brick and mortar out there in the future. The board—and I—are looking for someone with the experience and leadership skills to do that."

"I understand, Graham. I'm not qualified. My dad thinks since he and Cooper are old friends and their great-grandfathers practically built this town together, that you and I would strike a deal and shake on it."

Graham laughed. "The Gentlemen's Agreement is not dead, it just doesn't apply to this situation."

J.R. stood and extended his hand. "Thanks for your time and advice."

"Whoa, now, wait a minute. You haven't said what you want to do after graduation. I get the feeling you don't want to run with the titans of business and finance on Wall Street."

J.R. settled in his chair again. "Dad wants me to run our family's businesses, but he's not ready to retire. He wants me to get some experience, but he doesn't want me far from home—thus, the bank."

The kid sat there like a tortured knot of barbed wire. Jim, Sr. sure had done a number on him. J.R. was smart enough. A Longhorn education didn't earn itself, but it was clear his dad had been pulling the strings so long, the kid didn't know how or was too afraid to express what he wanted. He was a grown man, but his father had pounded him so far into ground with his own plans and dreams that he wasn't ready for real life and had no idea how to survive the cutthroat world of money.

Graham understood all that. He and his younger brother Brent had been pummeled with their dad's expectations to the point of brokenness. Graham survived well enough and thrashed his way through on his own terms. Brent's issues were only magnified by their father's pressure. He didn't survive at all.

"J.R., your dad's not here. You're about to graduate from college. What is it you want to do?"

"My girlfriend Stacey is an accounting major, but we discovered a couple years back that we both really like to teach, and we want to work with the disabled."

"As in children? I saw in the community paper where you'd taken some kids out to the ranch for horseback riding."

"Yes, that, but I'm talking about young adults. People who've aged out of the school system and are entering the workforce."

"Sounds like you're dealing with more mental issues than physical."

"A lot of our students have developmental delays. They live with their parents, but they want independence. We want to teach them to be as self-sufficient as possible and to manage their money and not be taken advantage of." He shifted in his seat. "We're also looking at ways to help teens who struggle with mental illness. Stacey's younger sister... she's bi-polar. It's been hard for her family. It never stops..."

J.R.'s words dropped away as wounded silence grew between them. Graham knew it was bound to come up.

"I miss Brent," J.R. said. "There's not a place in this town where a memory of all of us as kids doesn't hit me. I can't imagine how hard it is for you to be back here."

Graham nodded. "Some days it's rough."

"I see a lot of Brent in some of the things Stacey's sister deals with. I didn't recognize it back then."

"Stop right there. You were kids. We were all young. There's no way you could have or should have recognized that."

No, the people who should have known didn't do enough. The semi-retired dinosaur family doctor his dad took them to for strep throat and stitches wasn't equipped to diagnose the hidden and mysterious signs of a chemical imbalance or growing depression. An expert would have done that. But why find an expert when all the boy needed was a swift kick and an attitude adjustment?

Graham scooted forward, desperate to get back on track. "So what's the end game on your plan? Is someone going to pay you to do this full time?"

"I need more training. Stacey figured it out a while ago. She talked to her parents and is adding to her degree plan. But my dad... Can you imagine how he'd take this? *Boy, if you were bacon, you wouldn't even sizzle. I didn't pay for a fancy degree so you could teach Special Ed at the elementary school.*" J.R. barked out a sad laugh. "But you know my dad. He wouldn't be politically correct about it."

"Probably not." Graham knocked a pen around his desk with his index finger. "If you don't want to work for your dad, you need to man up and let him know."

"Isn't it my obligation to work for my family?"

"A lot of people would see it that way, but you also have an obligation to yourself. Sounds like this thing with your girl is gonna stick too. You all need to be happy, not just your dad."

"I know."

"Let me ask you again. Dream opportunity. What is it?"

J.R. didn't pause. "I want to develop a finance boot camp for people with intellectual disabilities. It can't be taught in a classroom. Students have to physically understand they're exchanging money for merchandise. My dad has all this property sitting there and, in our minds, we've built a camp for people to come and stay. Total immersion. Make money, spend money, save money."

"Impressive goal."

"Stacey wants a mental health support center component to the program too. A safe place where those with issues can attend a support group or a workshop, maybe take a class." J.R. let out a long, heavy sigh. "It's all a file folder full of ideas right now. Stacey's gone as far as to take a grant writing course, but we have a ways to go with funding."

"Send a proposal here. The board is always looking for ways to invest and get the bank's name on something. This year, they said it had to be something besides another scrolling marquis at the football stadium. They're ripe for diversity in our community involvement."

"Thanks, Graham, I will."

"I'm serious, J.R., this is business. I think you're missing the big picture. I believe there's a compromise with your dad. You have all the right ducks running around. Get them in a row and see what they can do for you. Do you understand?"

"I do. Thank you."

Graham stood and snatched his keys off his desk. "I have to grab some lunch and go see my dad." He paused and searched for the right words. "Thanks for talking about Brent. Some people act like it never happened—like he never happened. They're afraid to talk about him."

"I wouldn't forget him, Graham."

"Thanks." He twirled his keys around his finger. "I'll watch for more information. Get started. Do the work. Talk to your dad." He extended his hand. "I'll do everything I can for you."

THE FATHER-DAUGHTER PICNIC

J.R. stood and grasped his hand with far more determination than he had when he walked in the door.

Graham smiled. "Now *this* is a Gentlemen's Agreement."

THE WAS ONLY ONE thing that rattled Graham more than knowing a legion of fraud investigators was combing through all his work in Houston.

That one thing was visiting his dad.

He loved his father, but their relationship had been a nightmare for years. He didn't know exactly when he'd gotten crossways with the legendary Cooper Hollister, but it happened early, and they never managed to find a comfortable co-existence. *Your father is a fish*, his mother used to say, *and you and Brent are birds. You don't speak the same language, so it's hard for your father to know how to parent you.* But how hard could it be to love and encourage your sons, no matter what the species? Don't you just choose to give it your best shot? His mother and brother had been the connective tissue holding the four together. With them gone, there was no buffer between he and his dad. No alternating current to bind them together and off-set their natural tendency to repel each other.

And now this. The terrible accident that left his father with complicated injuries and many more questions than answers. Found on the trail during a cold snap in December, no one knew if he had a stroke and fell off his horse, or fell off his horse and had a stroke. Severely broken leg bones suggested his horse landed on him before it recovered and sprinted back to the barn. Coop's recollection of the event was as uneven as the long laceration that sliced his arm. The usually shrewd but likable sixty-five-year-old now waffled between melancholy and cantankerous on a daily basis.

Graham signed in and pressed the visitor pass onto his lapel. One glance past the double doors to the administrative wing showed no sign of Caroline Bishop. That woman didn't know anything about him, and she had no right to pass judgement on the time he spent with his dad. Where was she when he walked the halls at the regional hospital while Coop was bounced from floor to floor until it was safe to transfer him to rehab? Evaluate the damage, set the bones. Treat the stroke, test the brain. Advance to therapy, relapse to twenty-four-hour hospital care. Weeks had turned into months. The man stayed barely stable enough to begin to walk again. There seemed to be no end to the watch-and-wait.

Caroline Bishop knew nothing of his devotion to a father who cared so little for him and mistook him most days for his dead brother.

She was nothing but a thorn in his already wounded side—and, for some reason, she was sitting at Coop's bedside when he reached the room.

He ducked out of the way.

So he could eavesdrop.

While peeking around the door.

The official Ms. Bishop sat with a notepad. Long, dark hair swished across the back of her champagne-colored blouse. A gold hoop of tiny crystals dangled from her ear and played peek-a-boo with the sun that streamed through the window. His father seemed entranced by the specks of light they cast against his sheet. The woman was a first-class pain in his

THE FATHER-DAUGHTER PICNIC

backside, but she was also an exotic beauty that Graham found hard not to gawk at. Especially when she didn't know he was looking.

She scooted closer to the bed. "Can you tell me about today, Mr. Hollister?"

Coop pressed his left fist into the mattress and pushed himself to sit straighter. He then used the same hand to pull his weakened right arm to rest in his lap. Salt-and-pepper whiskers stuck out across his jawline, while his hair did its own thing in all directions. The therapists were supposed to be helping him with personal grooming. Obviously, that hadn't happened.

"Mr. Hollister? What happened today?"

"Nothin'," he declared and hitched his chin. "Not a darn thing."

"Well, that's the problem now, isn't it? *Nothin'* has happened in several days, and this morning you caused a ruckus in the exercise room."

"I want to go home."

"I know you do, but we have to make sure you're ready. When your care team met with you and your son, they set some very attainable goals for you, but you haven't been cooperating with your therapists."

Coop frowned and then his expression lightened. "Brent is here? I need to see him."

Ms. Bishop glanced at a page in her lap. "No, the meeting was last week and your doctors were in the meeting along with your son, Graham."

Coop nodded. "Yes, Graham."

"Everyone agrees you should be up and around on that leg, and you need to keep working to get that arm moving. Julian says you've been refusing to try to write or shave or comb your hair."

"My son Brent will help me when I get home."

"Yes, people can help you, and we'll send you home with all the equipment and assistance you need until you're all right on your own, but we can't even consider that until you start doing the work here." Her voice changed and carried the softness of a spring rain as she leaned closer and tried to pull information out of the grumpy old guy. "Julian also says you won't play your memory games with him on the tablet."

"I hate that thing."

"He said he tried games without the tablet and you wouldn't play those either."

Coop rested his head on the pillow and closed his eyes.

Ms. Bishop dropped her gaze for a second and then sat up as if with new resolve. "Mr. Hollister, please listen to me." She gave his arm a comforting pat. "I know you get agitated because that arm won't work like it used to. It's scary when you play those games because you can't remember things—like whether you're supposed to choose the red block or the green one. That's terrifying for you, but your memory will improve if you practice. That's all we're trying to do. Help you practice so you can go home."

Graham leaned in to hear their conversation over the noise in the hallway. That, and he wanted to take another look at the usually sharp-tongued administrator. She never spoke to *him* with such patience. Who knew there was such a warm heart under that frostbitten exterior?

Coop's weak arm shook as he tried to point. "Cards is the only game."

THE FATHER-DAUGHTER PICNIC

"We can do that," she answered. "I'll let Julian know you want to play cards."

"Already tried. He doesn't play Hold 'em."

"You want to play poker?"

Coop nodded.

"Why didn't you say so?" Caroline stood and smoothed her slacks across her distractingly curvy bottom. "I'll come by this time tomorrow with a clean deck. If you've accomplished two tasks from your daily routine list, we'll play a round."

"Why would I do that?"

"What do you mean? You said you wanted to play cards."

"I do, but you've got it backwards, missy. You don't settle up before you play. You settle up after you play. Why would I give you something up front? Especially since I'll win the game and you'll owe *me* something."

Ms. Bishop gripped the back of the chair. "I see."

"So what are the stakes?"

"I'm sorry, Mr. Hollister, I can't take your money."

"Oh, I'm talkin' milk money here. No serious cream."

She laughed and Graham wanted to, except that they'd hear him. That right there was the real Cooper Hollister. It was proof the old man was in there somewhere.

"Well, I do enjoy a rousing hand of Hold 'em, so what's your pleasure?" she asked. "Chocolate kisses? Lemon drops? Peanut clusters?"

"How about if I win, you leave me alone?"

Ms. Bishop stood straight and pressed an index finger against her full lips as she formed a retort. "How about if I win, you do your exercises so I don't have to discharge you for being a non-compliant patient?"

Coop smirked. "No problem."

She scooted the chair away from the bed. "Deal. I'll see you tomorrow."

Graham scrambled from the door and tried to look like he'd just arrived, except that he didn't know what that specifically looked like, and Ms. Bishop was still talking and not leaving.

So he was still standing in the hall like a goofball.

Graham heard her heels as she stepped toward the door. He took a couple steps of his own—backwards.

"Get some rest, Mr. Hollister. You have a lot of work to do."

Graham had intended to smile and nod as he passed the feisty administrator in the hall.

Instead, in true cartoon-character form, his shoes slid on the highly polished floor as he spun around and looked for a place to hide. Where? He didn't know. He hadn't thought it through.

Why? Because he was an idiot.

He dove into the alcove with the short and tall water fountains.

The fierce tapping of her heels grew closer as water splashed the side of his face.

"Mr. Hollister?"

"Yes." He jerked upright and tried to wipe the drops from his mouth. "Ms. Bishop. I'm on my way to visit my father."

"Nice of you to swing by this week. He's had a rough couple days."

Her words and the condescending way she clicked her pen closed brought his irritation to a new level. Forget how enticing

THE FATHER-DAUGHTER PICNIC

she looked or smelled. She didn't get to bully him every time they crossed paths.

"Look, Ms. Bishop, I don't know what I've done to offend you, but clearly, I've made my way onto your hit list. That stops today. I'd appreciate it if you'd refrain from making snide comments regarding the frequency of my visits here, and limit our conversations to the care of my father."

It felt good to brush past her and leave her spinning in his wake of fury.

"Mr. Hollister?"

"*What*?" he snapped and turned.

"I'd like to discuss your father's care, but since we obviously bring out the worst in each other, perhaps you can put me in contact with Brent. That's your brother, right? Your father mentions him quite often, but he's not in any of the paperwork. I've not seen him here either, and I'd like to talk to him."

"Well, that makes two of us, but I'm afraid it's not going to happen. Brent's been dead for three years."

Graham turned again and gripped the door frame to catch his breath. He didn't want to blurt it out like that, but he had. Saying it out loud sucked the fire out of him and made him lose a step as he tried to collect himself before seeing Coop. And she was standing behind him, now with more information. Information that hurt him far more to say than it did for her to hear. She didn't deserve to know his pain and certainly didn't get to turn the knife in his oozing wound.

"Mr. Hollister, wait, please."

He had no intention of waiting. She could stand in the hall, but he was going to see his dad.

He would have kept moving except that she touched him, put her hand right there on his back and warmed him in such a way he didn't want to squirm out of her reach.

And that was terrible, especially when he met her gaze. The intensity of her flat brown eyes morphed into more of a warm mug of cocoa than the hard, critical glare he usually found there.

"What now?"

"Mr. Hollister, we need to talk. I've got a fresh pot of coffee in my office. Come and sit with me for a minute?"

He'd only had the upper hand for a second.

CAROLINE WALKED INTO her office and motioned to the chair for Graham Hollister to take a seat. She took a cup from the stack on the cart. "Can I get you one?"

"No, thank you."

Huge relief. She didn't want to pour hot liquid into a small Styrofoam cup while he watched. She'd stepped in it big time when she'd popped off about his brother, and it left her shaky. No one deserved the pain of loss, and she certainly didn't want to add to his.

"I'm sorry about your brother," she said as she sat in her desk chair. "I had no idea."

He nodded.

It was fast, but it was there. A soft and vulnerable flash in his eyes, and the look of a man who'd been stabbed in the heart by grief. So fast, then it was gone, but she'd seen it, and she understood it. Suddenly, she and the pompous banker had something in common.

She searched for the appropriate thing to say as he fidgeted in his seat and eventually left it to look at the collage of pictures hung on the wall. Maybe bringing him into her personal space was a mistake, but they had to discuss his father's care, and she had to redeem herself for her embarrassing and pointed remarks about his brother.

"That's J.R. Hunt," he said.

Right there, that was it. The curious tilt of his head when he turned to look at her. The way his hair tickled the collar of his crisp white dress shirt. The familiar stance when he leaned ever-so-slightly forward to study the picture. Comforting one second, terrifying the next, and totally unexpected that he would strike such a similarity to... *Jason*.

Most disturbing? The exquisite inappropriateness that, for a flurry of nanoseconds, she would enjoy the living, breathing reminder.

She stood to join him by the photo and stumbled at the corner of her desk. "I'm sorry, what?"

He smiled. "It's J.R. Hunt."

Lightheaded from all her internal whirling, she steadied herself near his side. "Uh... Yes. Friend of yours?"

"Yeah, sure. Saw him this morning. Our families are longtime friends." He studied the other pictures of her volunteer work. "When was this one of you and J.R. taken?"

She remembered it well. Crazy with loneliness and terminally bored, she'd volunteered to help serve lunch the day J.R. organized a trail ride for disabled teens. Ava had loved every minute of being at the barn, and Bette was right. She wasn't going to be able to keep the girl from her horse obsession much longer.

"It was last fall at the Hunt's ranch. We had a patient here who was rehabbing from a car accident. J.R. knows the kid's family and set it all up. Animal therapy always turns out to be a good idea."

What she didn't tell him was that she cried all the way home while Ava slept. Missing her husband, sad he was gone, deeply grateful her daughter was well.

Graham swiped a hand through his dark hair and met her gaze for too long a moment. It propelled the awkwardness of them being alone in her office to a whole new level.

"Yep," he finally said and scurried like a nut-hunting squirrel to his chair. "J.R. has a lot of ideas."

Caroline scrambled a bit herself, and hit her seat with a rolling stop. Cooper Hollister's records appeared on her screen after a couple of clicks. "Mr. Hollister, your fath—"

"Hold up a sec." Control seemed to seep back into his bones as he sat straighter and a challenging glint returned to his deep blue gaze. "Can you call me Graham, please? Coop is already one Mr. Hollister too many. We've been stuck in this pattern for a while now, so let's switch it up. I'm Graham, you're Caroline."

Annoyance sent sparks of heat to her face. She'd let her guard down for one second and his arrogance had returned full force. If he thought one flirty and ill-advised eye-embrace was going to change things... "I think we're fine the way we are. No need to drop our level of professionalism."

"C'mon, Caroline, we snipe at each other every chance we get. We bypassed professionalism a ways back."

So much for their hint of a connection. There was no real *connecting* with this overbearing man, and she didn't want to keep sparring with him. "Fine. Mr. Hollis—excuse me, Graham. Your father is declining services and refusing to cooperate with his therapists."

"What does that mean and what are you doing about it?"

"It means he is refusing treatment and he's not doing the work as outlined in the treatment plan you both signed off on."

"And?"

"And that is unfortunate because there's every indication he can recover from the broken bones in his leg and walk normally again. He can also regain some use of that arm, but he has to participate in his therapy."

"What are you doing about it?"

"Look, Graham, we're pulling out all the stops here and trying everything, but right now he's taking up a bed and doing nothing. There's a waiting list of patients who value our programs and staff, and who truly desire to get better."

"What exactly are you threatening?"

"I'm not threatening anything, but we'll be forced to release him if he won't comply. You'll have to arrange for care at home and hope he can progress there as well as he might have progressed here."

Graham stood. "He's not leaving here until he's well. I suggest you find a way to motivate your people to step up their game and make that happen."

She put her hands up in mock surrender. "Fine. Throw your weight around, storm out, it doesn't matter. Whatever push-back negotiation trick you want to play will not change the facts. Your dad has to do the work."

"What work is that? Playing poker with you?"

Total. Jerk.

"You were eavesdropping? Why didn't you come in? Your input might have helped."

Anger creased the lines on his forehead. She could see it there and in the way he squeezed the back of the chair.

"My input means nothing. In fact, most of the time he thinks I'm my brother, and he'd rather visit with him than me."

His second show of vulnerability softened her ire and reached every gooey soft spot she had.

"Sit down a minute, Graham, and let's talk about that."

But it didn't look like he was going to relax and sit, and he sure wasn't going to do it because she asked.

He was right. For some reason, they were destined to pick at each other.

"About the neurological concerns," she said and glanced at the file, "I'm not his doctor, but I understand the prognosis is positive for his cognitive issues. The stroke damage is manageable with therapy. It's normal for there to be lapses and confusion in this area, and his behavior is consistent for someone with this type of event."

Graham didn't answer. Instead, he wandered to the window and adjusted the blinds to stare out into the parking lot.

"For example," she continued, "he remembers people, places and events, but he doesn't necessarily have it all in the right order. That's normal."

"He doesn't always recognize me, Caroline. He thinks I'm Brent sometimes."

THE FATHER-DAUGHTER PICNIC

No good answer came to mind. She didn't know the family dynamic or the elder Hollister's mental trauma associated with Brent's death. She did understand loss, and Mr. Hollister wasn't the only one hurt. Graham was in pain too. Against all her initial gut reaction to him, she finally got it. Graham didn't come because Cooper didn't see him.

What caused more pain than that?

"I don't have all the answers Graham, but that may help us. We won't release him as long as he needs us, but he has to try. I'm asking you to stick with it, spend more time here, and see if you can't encourage him to make a breakthrough."

She prepared for the blast and it didn't come.

"As for the poker," she added before he could form a response, "I enjoy working with patients, but my job leaves little time for direct involvement. When the opportunity came up with your dad, I jumped on it, because I thought it might help."

He flipped the blind closed. "Let me ask you something. What's the latest story he's told about his accident?"

"He talked about that today. He said he was out with his horse Maggie. Maggie pulled to a gate and he bent to unlatch it. He says there were some hogs up ahead near the path and the horse spooked. The dogs took off barking and your dad got caught up in the saddle horn when the horse stumbled. He said he fell off."

"Well, now, there's the problem." He headed for the door, but stopped in the middle of the room to plant his hands on his hips and shoot her a menacing glare. "I know how that story ends. He says he remembers everything, and wasn't worried because Brent or someone would be around to find him because the horse ran back to the barn. But we both know Brent wasn't going to come." He reached for the door. "Good luck with the game. My dad's a shark, but if you win, he'll make good on the bet."

"Oh, I plan to win. I want him back in active therapy and, with enough help, back on the trail with Maggie."

"Don't count on it." He turned the doorknob. "Maggie's gone too. He shot her himself because he loved her that much. Same way he unplugged my mother." He slumped against the door. "Same way he cut Brent from the rafters in the barn."

Bachelor #2 - Affectionate Adam and the Alarming Advance

Caroline plastered on a smile, but there was no denying this was the last place she wanted to be. She didn't usually go on semi-blind dates two nights in a row, but it just happened this way. Adam's nursing schedule didn't make it easy to meet people outside of his work, and left even less time for dating. Still, they'd sparked up some chemistry in their online chats and texts, and he seemed worth the effort. Being a medical professional was clearly a plus. Kids got sick, faked sick, and sometimes didn't seem sick when they really were sick. A nurse could come in handy with a six-year-old at home.

Mercifully, he'd texted to say he'd likely be called in before midnight to cover a shift. Would she mind meeting for coffee instead of dinner because he really wanted to meet her and didn't want to postpone?

He sent a heart emoji.

That beating pink heart was probably hiding a giant, flapping red flag, but she was so twisted up about all the Graham Hollister bombs going off in her head, she didn't have the energy to acknowledge it.

And it was coffee. It didn't have to lead to anything if she didn't want it to.

A coat of frosted lip balm, a swipe of illuminating powder, and she was good to go as she slid into a booth at Songbird's and watched the door.

"Oh, hey, girl!" There was a squeal. "*Hey!*"

Her friend Tammy Patty's voice hit her ears like a shrill whistle. Caroline turned in the booth to see the slightly plump ball of springtime exuberance and general good cheer exiting the bathroom and heading her way—with her three-month-old strapped to her chest.

Tammy was light and goodness. She loved Jesus and her family, and was the absolute go-to girlfriend for all things craft and bake sale related. Ava loved her, and often played with Tammy's girls. Any other day would have been a fine one to see Tammy and take advantage of her contagious positivity.

Today was not that day. Not after Graham. Not while waiting for a date.

"Hey, Tammy." She waved and hoped the busy mom would keep moving this time.

Nope.

Tammy stopped, her essence of mac and cheese and baby wipes settling in around her. She wore her daughter face-front, legs and arms dangling. Dressed in a red onesie, the precious cargo sported a tiny red headpiece, complete with a crimson feather and a splash of sequins. *Wow*. Tammy was ridin' the *First Baby of the New Year* train all the way to the station. Apparently, in Cardinal Point, it was a huge deal. The proclaimed *Royal Redbird Baby* was bathed in gifts and accolades, got to ride on parade floats, and made public appearances until the next New Year's baby arrived twelve months later.

THE FATHER-DAUGHTER PICNIC

Tammy seemed up for the challenge. She had on her stretchy jeans and a scoop-necked casual tee, but had added glittery silver Toms and a red, rhinestone pin in the shape of a crown.

She caught Caroline looking. "It's pretty, isn't it?" She rubbed the shiny piece.

"Was that part of the prize package?"

"Oh nooooo," Tammy sang out across three southern syllables. "I found this on eBay."

Caroline touched the baby's fuzzy red sock. "Hey, Scarlett," she cooed. The porcelain-skinned angel with the dusting of red hair wiggled under the attention.

Tammy brushed an auburn corkscrew curl away from her face. "We're not callin' her that anymore."

"You changed your baby's name?"

"Oh, heaven's no. It's Whit's fault. He wanted the middle name Roberta, after his mom. I said fine. Then, he started calling her Bertie because he thinks he's referencing the whole *Redbird Baby* thing."

Caroline glanced at the crimson hat perched on the side of the baby's head and nodded as if she understood. Any of it.

"Don't have the heart to remind the big lug that Bertie after his mom is B-E-R-T-I-E and the one he has in mind is B-I-R-D-I-E. If he doesn't figure it all out in a few days, I'll fix it."

"I love the name Scarlett," Caroline said, as if her two cents mattered. "It suits her."

"Yeah, well..." Tammy looked around for a chair because it was evident she couldn't slide into the booth wearing a baby. "Let's pray my linguist husband gets a clue. God help me, I love that man, but he doesn't have a great command of the English language."

"Huh." Caroline thought of Davey. "Must be an epidemic."

Tammy dragged the wooden chair to the table. "What's that?"

"I'll tell you later. And Tammy, I'd love to visit, but I'm expecting someone."

"I'll only be a minute. It's time to get the girls from ballet," she said and plopped into the chair. "I've been wondering how you are and I have a message for you." Tammy leaned her way and squashed Scarlett/Bertie/Birdie between herself and the table. "Wait. A. Minute." She jerked back when the baby grunted. "Ooops! Sorry, baby." She pushed her to the side to lean in again. "Forget the message. That's nighttime lipstick you're wearing." Her low, hoarse whisper was as funny as the eyes buggin' out of her head. "Are you waiting for a date?"

"Stop it, Tammy. It's not a date. It's coffee. It's... It's..."

"Oh, Lord, it's a date." Tammy pinched her forehead like she had a sudden brain freeze. "Bette told me this was happening and I couldn't believe it."

"You talked to Bette about this?"

"I ran into her and Ava at the store. She's worried about you."

"You talked about this in front of Ava?"

"No, darlin', of course not. I'm your friend. I only want you to be happy, but I do have concerns about you hooking up with men you met on the internet."

"Thank you, Tammy. That makes me feel really great about myself."

THE FATHER-DAUGHTER PICNIC 41

"Oh, I'm sorry, I didn't mean it like that. I'm saying you're a catch, darlin'. You don't need that. There are plenty of good men here in Cardinal Point. You'll find you one when the time is right."

"Spoken by someone who already has a good man. Forgive me if I think it's a harder than that."

Tammy sat back as her lower lip popped out in near pout.

Caroline checked the door. *Please be late, please be late...* She grabbed her compact and dusted on another layer. "You've got it made, Tammy. Whit loves you and the girls." She snapped it closed and tossed it in her bag. "You don't have to worry, but I do. I've read all the books and studies about girls who don't have a positive male influence in the home. There's some truth in there. I didn't have it. I don't want Ava to not have it. Even Jason didn't want her to not have it. It's up to me to find it for her."

Tammy reached out to touch her hand. "I get it. I do. But these things take time. You can't make this decision from a dating service."

"Bette says that too," Caroline huffed back, "but what she really means is let *her* take a stab at it because clearly, everyone has a better idea of what I need than I do." She pointed her gaze at the sleep-deprived, but happy wife and mother. "I suppose you have someone in mind too."

"Graham Hollister," she blurted on a whoosh of air as if she'd been trying to hold in the name.

"You've got to be kidding me." Caroline could literally feel the splotches of red exploding on her face and neck. *Pop! Pop! POW!*

No amount of powder was going to cover her clear embarrassment and irritation. "Does anyone care that this is my personal business? How much have you and Bette discussed this?"

Tammy tried to look away, but Caroline was faster. As quick as a soccer mom in a minivan, she grabbed her friend's ear and held on like they were two junior high sisters in a fight over clothes.

"*Ow, Ow, Ow*," Tammy screeched.

Caroline turned her loose and begged God to not let her date be standing in the doorway.

"I'm sorry," Tammy said and rubbed her ear. "But that man's hotter than a burning stump, and I don't see why you won't give him any consideration, but you're happy to entertain a parade of strangers from the World Wide Web."

"I don't have time for this right now, Tammy. Graham and I are oil and water. We both acknowledge we bring out the worst in each other."

"Have you ever actually talked to the man? Or are you still waging war against him simply because he doesn't act the way you think he should with his father?"

"I have talked to him and I can tell you he's not for me. I can't comment on the situation with his father. It's complicated."

Tammy slipped her finger into Scarlett's palm and squeezed her tiny hand. "So you've gotten to some history there? You should know Graham's a decent guy. Had some bad days, but a very decent guy."

Graham's haunting words played in her head again. *Same way he cut Brent from the rafters in the barn...* It made her stomach hurt and her heart thump out of rhythm for a couple beats. She'd have herself an empathetic cry for him when she got home, but right now, an uninvited Tammy crowded her table and Adam was on his way.

She pulled herself from the sad and desperate place in her soul where all deep mourning waited to suck her in and drown her.

"My friend will be here any minute. I can't talk about Graham now. He's a non-issue in my love life because he's arrogant and irritating." When she paused, a half-dozen of those irritating things came to mind. "He does this thing where he stands all cocky and plants his fists on his hips like I'll listen to every word he says if he'll just say it with enough force. Well, I don't respond to that. And I don't respond when a man steps too close and acts like he's doing me a favor by letting me sniff his cologne or... appreciate his eyes." The last few words fell away on what remaining breath she had left to support them. She mustered another round of air. "Graham Hollister needs to stay away from me."

"He does, does he?"

"Yes, he does."

"Oh my cheese and crackers." Tammy stood and started a giant, dramatic eye roll that didn't end until she scooted the chair away. "Do yourself a favor and send your date away if he ever gets here."

"Why would you say that?"

"You, my darlin', are attracted to Graham Hollister. You should explore that," she added with a heap of fake, innocent sugar. "I think you're a little smitten."

Irritation gushed through her veins so fast she didn't know how her head stayed attached. "That's crazy, Tammy. I feel nothing for Graham."

"Yep. Ya do. You're a smitten kitten."

Caroline chose to ignore her. Any other response would be inappropriate and possibly dangerous. "Didn't you say you had a message for me?"

"Oh yes. Whit said to mark your calendar for the last Saturday in April. It's the annual father-daughter picnic. He would like Ava to join him and the girls, if that's OK."

Caroline scrolled through the calendar on her phone. Numbers blurred as more raw emotion came from that deep, mournful place. She didn't know anything about an annual father-daughter picnic until that moment, but suddenly, it was too massive for her shredded emotions. Why didn't anyone realize this is exactly what her quest was about? She didn't want substitute fathers pitying her child. It was bad enough she had to find a replacement one. At least with her plan she could build a new family with a suitable candidate and Ava would have someone of her own.

And if Jason were alive, none of this nightmare would be necessary.

Despair took solid hold now, and swept her toward the sea.

Tammy leaned to capture her in a warm, sideways hug. "I didn't mean to hit a nerve, darlin'. I should have asked you at a less rushed time. Please know Whit's offer comes from the purest of places. His big ol' heart scoops up everything it its path."

THE FATHER-DAUGHTER PICNIC

An audible gasp got away from her as Tammy's hug dragged her back on shore. "I know. It's fine. I'm sure she'll be excited to go. Tell Whit I said thanks for the offer."

"Sure." She adjusted the carrier and smoothed Scarlett's hair. "How about lunch after church on Sunday?"

"Yes. Let's talk tomorrow."

"Oh yeah, we're talking tomorrow," Tammy said and turned to strut away with the *Royal Redbird Baby*. "You can count on it."

"Caroline? Caroline Bishop?"

Right on time.

She'd taken her eyes off the door, it was too late for more concealer, and her so-called nighttime lipstick evaporated a while ago.

Yep. She was ready.

The man stood near the booth with that worried *are you the right person* look on his face. Shorter than she imagined and only slightly like his profile picture, she wasn't sure either.

"Adam?"

"Yes. Hi."

She stood to shake hands because that's what she did. It was an introduction, after all, a first impression, the polite thing to do.

But Adam stepped way too far into her personal space for a first-time meeting and, well, took it someplace weird.

Musky cologne hit her nose as his lips met her cheek in an intimate hello. Taken aback, she tried to wriggle away. He tugged her hand until she moved forward instead of back. The awkward encounter ended with a deep sniffing sound in her ear. "Mmmmm..."

This wasn't a greeting. It was an assault.

"Adam, please." She jerked away.

"Sorry." True repentance and embarrassment seemed to cross his face. "I don't know what I was thinking." He slipped into the booth. "Please sit."

The beating pink heart emoji pounded in her head. He had boundary issues, to say the least. Was there something more dangerous lurking below? Or was he just a clumsy, overly-demonstrative cuddler?

The answer didn't matter because of Ava.

"I'm sorry, Adam. This isn't going to work. I have to go."

CAROLINE JUMPED IN the car and locked the doors. She fired up the engine and skidded out of Songbird's parking lot, only to pull in two driveways later and park at the back of the drugstore.

Out came the hand sanitizer.

A drop on her hands, a swipe across her neck and earlobe, a layer on the steering wheel she'd already touched—for added protection.

"Ew, ew, *ewwww*." She snapped the lid closed and waved her hands to dry them. "How could I have been so wrong on this one? I'm usually so good at weeding out the weirdos." She plucked her phone out of the console to text Bette.

Coffee's over. Disaster. She added a couple deranged emoji faces.

You didn't pinch your thigh, did you?

THE FATHER-DAUGHTER PICNIC

No. I'll be home to put Ava to bed. Have to go by work. Running in the drugstore. Need anything? She usually added a pink heart, but now that made her feel dirty.

Dark chocolate X2.

Caroline stepped out of the car and stalked toward the door as if on a mission. *2 bars?*

Bars, bags, wheelbarrows, whatever...

Caroline laughed and dropped the phone in her purse.

Within seven minutes, she was on her way again, having snagged the dark chocolate, and every dust-covered, plastic-wrapped deck of cards they had to offer.

She ached to go home and put the whole wretched day behind her. From her corporate boss that morning, to the recent coffee disaster, men had been trying to annihilate her last healthy nerve all day. But, of all the men who'd driven her batty that afternoon, Cooper Hollister made her want to pull her hair out the least. Graham's sad words had played in a steady loop in her ears, and left her with a bottomless, familiar chunk of pain in her gut. Beyond rationale, she needed to check in on the confused and hurting patient before she could rest.

Food service carts sat parked in the hallway and overflowed with discarded dinner. That day's turkey and dressing scented the air as gravy pooled on messy trays, and used cups of cranberry sauce congregated in a tub at the bottom of the rack.

Up ahead, Mr. Hollister made small steps into his room with a walker and the help of Julian.

That excited her more than she expected.

She rushed to his side. "Mr. Hollister! You're up."

The frail man paused with his stronger hand on the rail, while the other rested on the walker and did little to support him. He grimaced. "Don't go gettin' all excited about it, missy." His blue eyes sparkled. "And don't think this has anything to do with your motivational speech today either."

"I wouldn't dream of taking credit for your hard work. I'm only thrilled to see you on your feet."

"Humph. I've got to get out of here and back to my bank in case the Feds have followed my son to Cardinal Point."

Caroline looked at Julian. He shrugged. Apparently he didn't know about the Feds either.

Mr. Hollister pointed to the chair. "Let me sit up a while."

"Sure thing, Mr. H." Julian helped him ease onto the seat. "I'll be back. Behave yourself."

She stood in the middle of his room, now aware she had no real idea as to why she'd come. Yes, she wanted to check on him. He looked great. Better, actually, but it wasn't as if she could blurt out what she knew and hug him. Had she thought she could comfort him?

"I thought we were playing cards tomorrow," he said.

"We are." She cleared her throat. "I have new cards. A lot of them." She dug around in her purse. "I bought a new supply for the therapy room. Except for this deck with Texas landmarks. Those are for my daughter. She's learning to play rummy."

He nodded. "It's past supper time. Shouldn't you be home makin' meat loaf for your family or something?"

"Not tonight." She attempted a smile, but it died on her lips. Those days of dinner for her traditional family of three were over, and her attempts to recreate them for Ava were falling flat.

THE FATHER-DAUGHTER PICNIC

"How old is your girl?"

"Six. She's in first grade."

"Nice age. Still sweet, not too sassy yet. She like horses? You should bring her out to the ranch and let her ride."

"Yeah, that seems to be a recurring theme in our lives. I might have to take you up on it."

He moved in the chair and tugged at his dark green sweatpants. He looked her straight in the eye. "Are you going to stand there makin' chit-chat, or are you going to crack that deck?"

"I thoug—"

"Scoot that chair over." He pulled at the small side table. "C'mon. No strings. A game of Head's Up so we can size each other up for tomorrow's game when I win my freedom."

"You mean when you agree to buckle down and get to work so you can stay?"

He grunted.

Caroline shed the wrapper and turned the slick new cards in her hand.

He divided a handful of sweetener packets between them to use as chips. "You look tired," he said and caught her gaze in surprisingly genuine look of concern. "Like you might have spent a long day trying to put socks on a rooster."

That caught her off guard.

For less than a second.

"Don't bother trying to distract me," she said as she shuffled. "And, if I look tired, it's because I spent some of my day with you and your son. I wasn't trying to dress any barnyard creatures, though Graham can be a farm animal of a different kind at times."

The old man laughed until he wheezed.

She put down two cards to determine the dealer. His was higher. He hesitated and glanced at his arm.

"You won the deal fair and square," she said. "You can use that arm. Do what you can."

"All right," he said. "Let's get this done so you can get home to your family. Does your husband play poker too?"

"No. He doesn't. Rather, he didn't. I'm a—" She stopped short. The word *widow* never felt right to her, and jumped off her tongue every time she tried to use it. "My husband passed."

"Well," he said on a sigh. "For that I am truly sorry." He moved his weak arm to the table and wedged the deck between his fingers to he could deal with his sturdier hand. "If you don't mind my asking, what happened?"

"It was a very aggressive form of cancer. There was no time. It was quick." The phrases came fast from her mouth and skipped across her heart like flat stones on a pond. She'd repeated them so many times, she'd almost learned how to say them without aggravating the open wound. Almost.

"You were lucky." His tone surprised her. "Took my wife three years to die."

He was right, but that didn't mean it made it any better. Her appreciation for a quick death was still tinged with the memory of the suffocating race to find help when there was none to be found. Each remembrance heaped on another layer of guilt and pain about Ava, who was so little, and so totally lost in the chaos and destruction.

Coop offered the opening sugar packets, made an awkward shuffling attempt, and burned the top card. "You're not a native redbird, are you?"

THE FATHER-DAUGHTER PICNIC

"I'm sorry, a what?" She tossed in her bet and picked up the two cards he dealt.

"You're not from around here."

"Oh. No. I'm from south of here. I came to Cardinal Point for the job."

"Your parents still there?" He raised the bet, a daring pre-flop action in a friendly game over multi-colored packets.

She matched it. "No. They're gone." She didn't offer any more information and didn't need to. If he thought she looked tired before, a personal discussion about her absent father and certifiable mother would have taken her beyond exhausted. "But, speaking of family, I did ask Graham about Brent today." She paused. "You've mentioned him, but there was no contact information in your file. I didn't realize you'd lost a son."

Coop's poker face remained the same as he let the statement pass by. "You talked to Graham." He smirked. "Did he tell you about the Feds?"

Curiosity nudged her to explore the whole *Feds* reference. Instead, she kept her eye on the big picture goal of keeping him in therapy, and didn't let her mind wander far from the game. "No, he didn't. We talked about you, and how you're going to start working harder to get out of here."

"Yeah, I'm working on that right now." He placed the first three community cards face-up between them. "See how hard I'm working?"

Caroline glanced at those three cards and the ones in her hand. It wasn't pretty, but she had him already with an unusually early straight.

Coop flinched. He knew it too. "Well, if that don't beat all..." He tapped the table as he passed.

The words were in her head again, raw and heartbreaking. *Same way he cut Brent from the rafters in the barn.*

She put down her cards and reached to touch his arm. "Thanks for the game and the visit, Mr. Hollister. Get some rest. We'll play tomorrow."

Candidate #2 - The Green Go-Getter

As Monday mornings went, this one was drearier than most. Graham clicked on the lamp in his office and shuffled through a stack of paper. He'd intended to clear his cluttered brain on the trail with Jasper—Maggie's first foal who'd tossed his dad—but a muddy ride on that green-broke colt didn't seem like the best idea in the thunderstorm that hit the ranch in the pre-dawn hours. He'd get to the ride later and spend some time in the old barn. There, in the quiet, he'd re-hash a weekend's worth of frenzied communication with his lawyer in Houston, and then work through the situation with his dad. Seems Coop spent Saturday and Sunday in a series of agitated episodes because one Ms. Caroline Bishop was whoopin' his hide in every game of Hold 'em they played. As his Nana would say, *well, bless her stony heart*, for getting the old man up and moving. Nothing motivated Coop Hollister more than competition. He'd go to physical therapy now and jog the halls to spite her, all so he could dance out the front door when he finally beat her.

That, he supposed, was the genius in the prickly administrator's plan. She'd played them both well, forcing Graham to blurt out private details about Brent. She'd skimmed along the top of their family pain until the scab came loose and he'd revealed a fragment of their torture.

Death, dying, dysfunction. He'd spewed it all right there in her office doorway.

And that's why he'd find himself in that old barn. Because somewhere in between all that pain and misery was something good. A happy memory of Brent's bright smile and tousled dirty blond hair. A glimpse of a lanky kid on a paint horse, riding the trail with him and the Hunt boys, and slinging bales of hay into the loft. There was a life, the whole life of a healthy and well-adjusted boy—until it became clear he wasn't.

Brent lived in that barn. Brent died in that barn. Somehow Graham had to reconcile the two.

Three years of numbness was wearing off. It'd been easy to ignore the pain as he hid in his office miles away and focused on his career while his dad sat on his pontifical perch and ran the bank. Now they were on a face-to-face basis. Coop struggled to make his way back from the brink of death, and Graham struggled to get away from a town he'd wanted to leave forever.

So, he'd be in the old barn, delving into hurt, and trying to piece his life back together.

There where Brent died.

But first.

First, he had to focus on the wisp of a woman who floated into his office and shook his hand like a confident lion. No nonsense, no make-up, no games. The dynamic, mid-thirties Amelia Green took a seat and pushed her long, neat braid off her shoulder as if she meant business.

By the end of the basic interview, it was clear she had skills. Adequately qualified and a self-proclaimed environmentalist, the higher-ups would probably love her progressive planet-loving style because it would make them look

THE FATHER-DAUGHTER PICNIC 55

forward-thinking. But was she up for the challenge in Cardinal Point? Forget going paperless. He couldn't even get his dad's assistant to use the two-sided function on the copier. The woman still printed out e-mails and showed them to him as if he hadn't already seen them in his inbox the day before.

Graham closed his laptop as Amelia's credentials faded to black on the screen. "Do you have any questions for me?"

"Yes, thank you for asking." She sat straighter in her chair. "As I said, I have a passion for the environment and, whenever possible, I think it's important for financial institutions to be involved in the community that supports them. How does the bank participate in this way?"

"We're a sponsor of the Cardinal Point Wildflower Festival. It's an eco-friendly event with representatives who have booths on everything from soil and water conservation to the continued beautification of Texas highways."

She smiled. "That's very nice. But being environmentally conscious goes beyond solar panels and energy efficient lighting at the branch office. It involves the bank itself making wise and ethical investment decisions in what it uses the community's deposits to support. For example, is your bank the funding source for the deforestation out by the freeway where the new shopping center's going to be?"

Well.

Graham pulled a jaw muscle trying to keep his smile within reason. Not because he thought she was that outrageous, but because if this is what got her riled up, she'd be none too pleased to know the bank's one recycle bin was currently being used as a trap in the break room because an armadillo kept slipping in with the nighttime cleaning staff.

"I'll be honest with you, Ms. Green. Based on your experience and expertise, you're qualified for this position. If you really want this job, I can recommend you to the next round of interviews with the board—based on your qualifications. As for your other interests, the board does want to incite positive change and growth in Cardinal Point, but you'll have to get there with the *catch more flies with honey than vinegar* approach."

She nodded. "Understood."

He stood and extended his hand. "Shoot me an e-mail and let me know if you want to go on."

Silence swept the room with the soft click of the door behind her. The quiet only sounded this loud when he didn't want to be alone with it. Lawyers, investigators, and all the other people in his life paraded through his head again and demanded attention.

He didn't want to deal with them.

He stuffed his laptop into his bag and grabbed his keys. The low rumble of thunder in the distance told him the storm hadn't passed. He'd visit Coop and try to smooth his ruffled feathers while he waited for the weather to clear.

His dad's assistant stumbled into his office and waved a yardstick as she tried to catch her breath. "Graham, come quick!"

"What's wrong?" Images of unthinkable bank-related emergencies raced through his mind.

"It's the armadillo," she said on a gasp. "We think we got him."

THE FATHER-DAUGHTER PICNIC

GRAHAM TOSSED HIS SUIT jacket in the trunk and headed out. Armadillo wrangling? Really? All he had to do was push the recycle bin to the door and let the creature wander out. Remarkable that no one else was willing to do it. It would come back that night anyway since the cleaning staff tended to prop the door at night while they worked.

Yes. They propped a door open. *At a bank.*

He wiped away a trickle of sweat. "I'm never going to get this place straightened out, am I? And I'm never going to get my life back and go home either, right?"

He supposed the questions in the empty car were directed to the God of his childhood whom he was sure used to listen, but now knew had ignored him for years. He'd even gone to church yesterday, mostly for the sake of appearance, but also to give the Big Guy one more shot. There was no peace while he sat there and avoided eye contact with Jim Hunt, Sr., whose only concern seemed to be to track him down and question him about J.R. and the bank position. No words of wisdom from the pulpit made him feel any better about his dad or Brent or his job.

Or that abrasive Caroline Bishop who'd made his headache come roaring back when he saw her standing at the back of the sanctuary during the offering. If she saw him, she didn't act like it.

Raindrops dotted his business-blue dress shirt as he darted toward the building to sign in. He breezed past the nurse's station with his laptop. The last thing he expected when he reached Coop's door was laughter. A child's laughter. He stepped back to make sure he had the right room.

Coop was hunched over a small table with cards fanned in front of his face and a pillow stuffed under his weak arm. A tiny kid with dark hair and pink tennis shoes sat with her legs dangling from a metal folding chair. Neither seemed a bit interested in his arrival.

"Dad?"

"Hold on," Coop replied without looking up. He lowered his cards and leaned in. "Now you draw," he told the girl.

Narrow fingers with chipped purple polish plucked one card from the pile in the middle. She looked up at Graham through a fringe of dark lashes. He knew this kid. But from where?

Coop adjusted his pillow. "Now. Does that card match anything you have?"

It took a while, but she finally nodded as she maneuvered the new card into the awkward stack in her hands.

"Do you have three of a kind? Can you put anything down?"

"Ummm... No. Not yet."

Graham practically tripped over himself to get closer. "Wait," he said and pointed out the partially hidden three of hearts. "This goes with those, right."

She frowned as she looked again. "Right."

Few things were more fun than watching her lay down those cards on Coop.

"Good job," he said.

She turned her full appreciation on him by way of a bright and triumphant smile. "Thanks, Mr. Graham."

THE FATHER-DAUGHTER PICNIC

Heart. Stolen.

Wait. Mr. Graham?

Oh... *Ava*. "You're welcome," he said and glanced out the door for Bette, the eccentric but entertaining woman who always brought her to the bank. "What's going on here, Dad?"

"What's it look like? Ava's learning to play rummy. It's not even noon. Who's minding the bank?"

"I'm pretty sure there's a small animal in charge."

"What?"

"Nothing."

"I'm back." Caroline hurried into the room and stopped so fast in her tracks at the sight of him she almost tumbled forward.

Yeah. This wasn't weird at all.

A hint of agitation crossed his dad's face. "Are we playing cards or not, little lady? You need to discard."

Ava sucked in her bottom lip as her hand shook with indecision. She glanced up at him for guidance. Her distressed *what do I do?* face propelled him into protective mode. No kid this young deserved a beating in the *Coop Hollister School of Intimidation*.

Caroline stepped forward, but everything in his body language must have waved her off. Daring, he knew, but Caroline didn't like him anyway, and he and Ava were apparently old friends. He had this.

He set his computer aside and dropped to his haunches. "You want to discard this one," he said. "You don't have anything to match the queen of spades and she's worth a lot of points. It's OK to let her go because you don't want to be caught with her if your opponent goes out."

Coop grunted.

Ava considered his words. The strategy may have been over her head, but the kid had brains and would get it all eventually. She'd been holding her own before he got there.

She looked at him with complete and utter trust and tossed the queen.

"Good work," he said. He stood and made his way to the ugly visitor chair in the corner. "Morning, Caroline."

"Hi, Graham," she said with a strained smile. "Didn't expect to see you this morning."

He acted like he was looking at his phone rather than the way she filled out her blouse. "Just thought I'd enjoy a visit with my dad."

She nudged Ava out of the chair. "C'mon, baby, we need to get you to the dentist."

Coop threw down his cards. "Doesn't anybody respect a game of rummy around here?"

Caroline took Ava's backpack and duck-covered rain slicker off the hook by the door. "I'll be back later for our regular game. You need to head to therapy."

"Mama, what's a hustler?"

Caroline turned a cool glare on the ornery old man. "I leave you alone for five minutes and this is what you teach her?"

Ava laughed and glanced at Graham as if he were in on the joke when, clearly, he was no part of this cozy... Whatever it was.

"I'm not hustling you, Mr. Hollister. We had a bet and I happen to be winning fair and square every day."

"Not today," he said with a grunt. "Today's the day I get you."

THE FATHER-DAUGHTER PICNIC

"That's fine," she said and winked down at her daughter with a smug smile. "You try to get me." She brushed Ava's bangs away from her eyes. "What do you say to Mr. Hollister?"

"Thanks, Mr. Hollister. Thanks, Mr. Graham. See you at the bank."

He returned a decidedly goofy grin. "I'll pop the popcorn. And maybe you can meet the armadillo."

"You have an armadillo?"

"I'm afraid I do."

"She doesn't need to meet an armadillo, Graham. Armadillos carry leprosy."

"Mama, what's leprosy?"

Coop pounded the table. "Everybody stop a minute. Graham, I'm glad you're here."

Shocker. He'd barely acknowledged his presence until then. "What it is, Dad?"

"I need you to take Ava and her mother to the barn. It's high time the girl learned to ride."

Caroline pulled her daughter close, as if they'd been threatened. "That's not necessary, Mr. Hollister."

"Let the girl have her horse," Coop ordered as if he had any say. "It's all she talks about when she's here."

Graham stood and made his way toward them. Had there been conversations? Or was Coop drifting into some clouded recollection of recent events? He met Caroline's gaze. "Sure, Dad. If they want to go to the barn, I'll make it happen."

"Let her pick a horse for herself," Coop continued. "I'm thinking Blossom or Marigold. They're gentle mares. Set her up with everything she needs and tell Miguel to start lessons."

Caroline relaxed. "Thank you, Mr. Hollister. We'll work it out."

Graham knew she meant it wasn't going to happen.

But Ava had already heard. "Can we go now? Please?"

There was squealing involved.

"It's too wet today," Graham offered. "We'll talk about it some more."

Coop hit the table again. "What's to talk about? Do it tomorrow."

"Can we, Mama?"

"I'm sure Graham is busy at the bank and I have to check my calendar for what we have after school."

"Are you, Mr. Graham? Are you busy at the bank?"

He wasn't going to lie. He had nothing. "I'm free."

"It's a date," Coop declared.

Caroline cringed. "Oh good," she mumbled and pinned him with a glare. "A date with a horse. And a horse's—"

"Nice," Graham said. "Very nice."

Ava swayed between them and brushed his hand with hers as if she wanted to take hold. She lingered like a kitten who craved attention while it pressed against his side. Her deep brown gaze met his and there was that smile again. The one that had run off with his heart.

Caroline seemed uncomfortable with their connection at first, but appeared to become oddly content with it as she surrendered with a smile.

Graham's gut reacted with unexpected joy.

These women were dangerous.

"Let's go, baby." Caroline dragged her toward the door.

"Oh no!" Ava wailed with obvious despair.

THE FATHER-DAUGHTER PICNIC

"What's the matter?"

"Mr. Graham? Am I going to get to meet my horse before the Feds come to get you?"

YOUR DESTINATION IS on the right.

You have arrived at your destination.

Caroline growled at her phone. "I know, I know, I know."

"What's the matter, Mama?"

Caroline glanced in the rearview mirror at her daughter's expectant gaze. "Nothing."

"Are we lost?"

"No, baby. We're not lost."

How could they ever get lost? The entrance to Coop's house could be seen from a mile away. The name *Hollister* arched across the driveway, cut out in bronze-colored metal with intricate western detail, and set on two tall poles.

Ava giggled in the backseat and stretched to see the matching giant planters on either side. "Those flowers are pretty."

"Yes, they are."

"Is this the way to the barn?"

"I think it's the way to the house."

"And then the barn where I get to pick a horse?"

Caroline smiled on the outside.

Inside, she raged against that old coot who'd made promises to her daughter with no thought of how those promises would be kept. Ava didn't need a horse. Caroline couldn't pay for a horse and all that went with it. For twenty-four hours, her daughter had been as happy and excited as she'd ever been. She'd even asked Bette to braid her hair like the girl riders she'd seen on TV. Caroline would have an ugly mess to clean up later when Ava realized she wasn't getting the horse that Coop went on about.

Pecan trees lined the final stretch of the long driveway. The large house came into view through the passing rails of a bright white fence. From the soaring porch columns to the massive, bougainvillea-accented breezeway, the home proclaimed its old Texas money and historic southern charm. There was something nostalgic and dreamy about the stately shuttered windows and second story balconies that no doubt concealed large, airy bedrooms with gently worn wooden floors.

"Do you think Mr. Graham is here?" Ava twisted in her seat and tugged at her shoulder strap. "Where is he?"

"I'm sure he's here," Caroline said as she slowed. "This is where he said to meet him."

"Text him," she said.

"I will, but can I please stop the car?"

Movement near a column caught her eye as Graham—at least she thought it was Graham—got up from a large double rocker. He stretched, glanced at his phone, and then pushed it into the back pocket of his well-worn, tight-fitting jeans. Again, this was Graham? The stuffy banker she'd seen only in suits now sported an old Mighty Fighting Redbirds T-shirt and a pair of boots.

He bypassed the wide steps and hopped off the porch as he pointed to where she should park.

And there it was again.

THE FATHER-DAUGHTER PICNIC

Something in that jump. Something in his gait. Something in the way he came to her side of the car and reached for the door.

It was something like Jason and it alarmed and disarmed her every time she saw it.

"Any trouble finding the place?"

"No, not at all." She grabbed her sunglasses as she half tumbled out the door.

He held her arm to steady her.

She caught her loose, gauzy shirt in the door as she tried to close it herself. The force yanked her against the window and pulled the blouse halfway up her back.

Good thing she had a cami underneath.

There were several things she could have said or done, and she probably should have just laughed at her clumsiness as she freed herself. Instead, she glanced at his boots and let her gaze travel the full length of his body and stop at his head. "What, no hat?"

"I have a hat." He pulled a ball cap from his back pocket and positioned it on his head. The *Cardinal Point Farm & Feed* logo stood out in stark white against a blaze of red. He grinned and tilted his head. "Oh wait," he said with a teasing smirk. "You're disappointed. You expected a cowboy hat. I have several. You want me to get one? Is that what you want?"

Now she was the one who was a blaze of red. Totally. She could feel the flames creep up her neck and race to the ends of her hair.

"Mama!" Ava pounded the window. "Get me out!"

"Good Lord," she mumbled as she darted around the car. "Coming!"

Graham was close behind. "Is she stuck in there?"

"No, it's the child safety lock on the door. Can't get out from the inside."

"Wow," he said. "Like a police car?"

"Yes, I suppose. I haven't been in the back of a police car, but now I know you have."

"Stuff happens," he said as Ava bounded out and grabbed his hand.

"Hey, Mr. Graham. Where's the barn?"

"That way," he said and pointed to a golf cart. "Hop on."

Terror seized Caroline by the throat like a hungry panther taking down prey. Her baby might fly right out of that death-trap. "Can't we walk?" she begged. "How far can it be?"

"I guess we can, but the cart will save time. Plus there are some muddy spots from all the rain."

"Ava's never been on one of those. Is there a seatbelt?"

"Um... I hope not," he said with a smirk. "Where's the fun in that?"

Ava jumped on the back bench seat while Graham got in and took the wheel.

Caroline prepared to rescue her child from certain death or dismemberment. "C'mon, Ava, don't you want to walk?"

"No, thank you," she said and hugged the rail.

Graham patted the passenger seat. "Get in the cart, Caroline. We'll make seven miles per hour. Ten tops. She'll be fine."

She did what he asked and hated him for it. She hated herself more for being a scaredy-cat. When had that happened? She'd been fun at some point, even adventurous. When did a golf cart become such a threat?

THE FATHER-DAUGHTER PICNIC

Graham stretched his arm across the back of the seat and turned to Ava. "Here are the rules, kid. Keep one hand on the bar at all times, and don't hop off until we're completely stopped and I say it's OK. Got it?"

"Got it."

Caroline's stomach jiggled a little when he smiled and winked at her daughter. It churned out of control when Ava smiled back with her whole heart.

Then her precious baby's expression turned to hurt.

Caroline flung her arm across Graham's chest. "Wait! Don't go yet."

Graham rested his hands on the wheel. "I'm not."

"What's the matter, Ava?"

"Nothing." She turned away.

"Are you sick?"

"No, Mama, I'll tell you later."

"Tell me now. We can leave if you're not feeling well."

Ava looked at Graham and then widened her eyes at her mother like an embarrassed teenager. "I don't want to go home. I want to meet my horse." She turned in the seat. "Mr. Graham can I hop off?"

"Sure."

Ava made a respectable dismount and hurried to her side. The dark braid dangled at her daughter's back as she wrapped an arm around Caroline's neck and pulled her head down for a private word.

"What is it, baby?"

Warm breath tickled her ear. "I miss my daddy."

CAROLINE RUSHED TO the water fountain along the wall in the massive aluminum barn as Ava darted off to explore. "Don't go too far," she commanded, and then tried to keep sight of that long, dark braid as it swished across her daughter's back.

The recent cart ride was a blur, and she had yet to right herself from Ava's comment. Sure, the girl missed her dad. That's what spurred Caroline's exhaustive search for a partner. But the fact that she so acutely felt the pain in the presence of Graham Hollister disturbed her. Why? Because it mirrored her own confusion and ache when she was around him. What was it that drew them both to him like needy baby ducks? It infuriated her to know they both felt it.

Despite Bette and Tammy singing his praises, the guy was clearly all wrong for them. Then again, so were Davey and Adam and all the other deviant clowns she'd been conversing with online. And it was a little sad and unnerving that it was glimpses of Jason she saw in him. They were nothing alike. Jason was leisurely spring walks in the rain, Saturday morning farmer's markets, and feeding the homeless with the city outreach. Banker-slash-cowboy Graham was money, excess, and arrogance. The barn alone probably cost more than any house she'd ever own.

"Caroline, are you all right?"

She spun to meet Graham's gaze and tuck her sunglasses into the front of her cami. "Yes. I'm fine. Why?"

"Look. Despite my father's current condition, this is a safe and well-managed barn. Miguel is the best there is. This should be fun for you and Ava. You should be having a good time, but if you're uncomfort—"

"I know. I'm sorry. I appreciate all this." She squeezed her eyes shut and covered her face with both hands before she took a breath and tried to talk again. "It's mom stuff and kid stuff and life stuff and I need to forget about all the stuff for a minute and... I don't know."

He stepped closer and touched her arm. "I'm not going to let anything happen to your daughter. She's safe here."

If only she had a guarantee that were true. Once upon a time she'd loved and cherished with everything she had. She'd lost it all. The thought of anything happening to her daughter after all they'd been through... It was way too much for her mortal mother's mind to comprehend.

Warmth seeped into her skin under his hand. It both startled and comforted her. When she looked at where his fingers pressed into her arm, he snatched them away.

He shoved his hand in his pocket as if to show he wouldn't do it again.

That made it worse. He was trying to help. Trying to put her at ease.

She was overreacting like a child.

"I do appreciate it, Graham. I know she's safe, but I have no experience with any of this. I have no idea where Ava developed her interest in horses."

He shrugged. "Does it matter? She's having fun. I thought you were going to forget about all the stuff for a minute."

"I am." She scanned the building. Thoughts of Brent popped into her head. This couldn't be the place where he died. Could it? She dismissed the painful and morbid question. "This isn't a barn, by the way. It's a luxury hotel for livestock."

"Yep," he agreed. "My dad redid everything about eight years ago. It's all modernized. Those stalls are custom tongue and groove panels made from treated pine. There are giant fans for summer and heat lamps for the cold, but Miguel's quarters and the office are fully heated and air conditioned.

"Amazing. All the comforts of home." She studied the pipe running above the stalls. "What's that?"

"Fly spray."

"You're telling me these pampered ponies don't even have to swish their own tails to shoo away flies?"

"Not if they don't want to."

"Well, when I heard barn, I thought wood and hay and pitchforks and scary spider webs in the corners."

"We have that too," he said. "It's a classic. We can put you on a horse and ride around the farm."

"I don't know about that. I know your father means well, but I'm not sure this is for us."

Ava wasn't helping her argument. From the minute Graham parked the cart and gave her permission to hop off, she'd run the length of the colossal structure with what could only be described as wild abandon and unbridled joy. She'd stopped at every stall and traced every letter on every name plate and said hello to every horse.

She came running to Graham's side. "Are all these horses yours, Mr. Graham?"

THE FATHER-DAUGHTER PICNIC 71

"No. We board horses for other people, but ours are all going to be at the other end."

"Where are Blossom and Marigold?"

"Keep looking. They're here."

"So which one is your horse?" Caroline asked as they tried to keep up with Ava.

"I think Jasper and I have established a rapport."

"Your dad mentioned a horse named Jasper. I was going to ask you about it because he hasn't said anything about Maggie in a while."

"That's progress, then. Jasper is the horse he was riding when he had his accident. The fog must be clearing." He slowed beside her. "Hold up a minute. I wanted to ask you something about you and my dad."

She came to an abrupt stop. She didn't much like the sound of that. "Excuse me?"

"Nothing like that. Geeze, Caroline. Not everything is a confrontation or an accusation."

She clasped her hands behind her back and waited.

"Yesterday, when I was there," he started, "it seemed like you'd been spending a lot of time with him. There was all this familiarity with Ava. I was kinda... shocked. My father is a hard, driven man, and yesterday he looked like some cuddly grandpa. Bristly, but cuddly too. I thought you were playing cards. When did you all become such buddies?"

"We played cards and I won. I was on a roll and didn't want to stop the progress. I said I'd keep coming, but then it was the weekend so I brought Ava. Didn't take long to beat him and he's been going to therapy. As for Ava, she's six. She expects only kindness so that's what she gets." She trapped a wood chip with her foot and kicked it aside. "On Sunday, they played Go Fish for an hour while I did paperwork in the corner. They talked about everything from bad mosquito bites to why your father had hair poking out of his ears. It was classic. And perfect."

It was obvious Graham couldn't picture it. His face was a total mask of disbelief. "All right," he finally said. "If you say so. But, be warned. My father always has an ulterior motive."

She took off walking. "Well, I'm not too happy he got me into *this*, but, in general, I like to talk to him. Everyone in that place has a story, Graham. They're old and they're sick, but they had lives, and loves, and jobs, and they're desperate to talk to someone about it. It's one of the reasons I love my job."

"I'm not knocking or questioning any of that," he said as he caught up to her. "But this is my dad. He once turned out the blue-ribbon rabbits Brent raised for the livestock show because one of them got loose in the house and chewed through his television cord. Brent never got over that loss. My father's not a nice guy, Caroline."

She stopped again. How she ever got between these two damaged and dysfunctional men would forever be a mystery. "I'm sorry, Graham. I don't know what to say. Maybe he's changed."

"I found them!" Ava's voice echoed in the large space as she ran. "They're here. C'mon."

Graham checked his phone. "Miguel should be here any minute."

Caroline held her breath while Graham made the introductions.

THE FATHER-DAUGHTER PICNIC

"This is Marigold," he said to Ava. "She's a red mare. That's Blossom next door. She's a blue roan. Either would make a fine horse for you."

"You must be Ms. Bishop."

Caroline greeted a short and stocky fifty-something-year-old man. Deep lines etched his olive-skinned faced, likely from hours in the sun.

"Call me Caroline. Thanks for taking the time to help Ava."

"Noooo problem," he said and wiped his hands on a small towel he pulled from his back pocket. "Mr. Hollister said fix her up, so that's what I'm going to do because he's the boss."

"I appreciate it, but I think Mr. Hollister is getting ahead of himself."

Miguel smiled so wide his twinkling brown eyes nearly disappeared. "We'll see," he said and joined Ava at the stall. "Which one will it be, Miss Ava?"

Graham greeted Miguel. "Ava, this is Miguel. You have to listen to everything he says, understand?"

"Yes, sir."

Caroline wasn't overjoyed about any of this, but when her first-grader confidently used her manners, it made her giddy with pride.

Miguel took two large brushes from a nearby shelf and grabbed a long strap of some kind off a hook. "Who's it gonna be?"

Ava took a step back. Then another. She motioned toward the end of the barn. "What's that over there?"

Miguel scratched his head. "The grooming area?"

"Yes," she said softly. "There's a horse over there. Can I meet that one?"

"Ah... Tilly. I took her over there a while ago because she needs to stretch her legs. Thought I might go for a ride when we're done here."

Caroline didn't recall a horse there when they walked up. "When did you see Tilly, Ava?"

"When we first got here and I ran all the way to the end and back."

Oh great. She'd been watching Ava, but somehow missed the child being alone with a loose horse that could have trampled her to death.

Miguel and Ava forged ahead. What had looked like anxiety and disappointment in her eyes with the other horses turned to excitement at the sight of the massive creature in the grooming bay. Ava approached with no apprehension and spoke to the mare.

Caroline gasped. She didn't know the first thing about horses, but she knew a magnificent palomino when she saw one. The golden color, the muscular body, the shiny white-blonde mane. A creamy stripe on her face completed the perfect animal. A beauty. A huge, powerful beauty that was probably the pride and joy of some other happy and experienced horsewoman.

"She's very pretty, Ava, but I'm sure Tilly has an owner. C'mon back this way. I don't think she's available."

Graham stepped to her side. "It's all right, Caroline, she's one of ours."

"You're not helping," she ground out between clenched teeth. "That beast is too big for her. That is not a starter horse for a six-year-old."

"She's a gentle, well-mannered, well-trained horse. Ava likes her."

"Well, Ava needs to get back over here to the horsey senior citizen department and choose between Marigold and Blossom."

Graham laughed. "C'mon, do you really want me to bust this up? See how relaxed Tilly is around her?"

"Please, Graham, Ava only wants that horse because it looks like one of her yellow pony toys with the flaxen mane. A horse is a horse is a horse."

Graham crossed his arms as if he took offense. "A horse is *not* a horse is a horse is a horse." He paused to wipe sweat from his brow with the bottom of his shirt and then met her constant gaze. "All right. I'll try to get her to reconsider one of the old ladies."

But while they'd been talking about it, Miguel had already handed Ava the brush with a strap. "First things first. Slip your hand in there and hold on. You need to get to know each other and that starts with a good brushing. Start here at her shoulder area. I'll fetch you a step stool in a minute and you can brush the saddle area. That's very important."

Ava's hand looked tiny against the horse's massive side, but she mimicked Miguel's movements and looked completely natural as she worked.

As if to show her appreciation, Tilly turned her head toward Ava.

Caroline lost her breath.

"She likes you," Miguel said.

Ava laughed. "Can I pet her?" She reached for her face.

"Right here," Miguel said. "Scratch her neck."

Tilly all but nuzzled her. That, Caroline supposed, was the equivalent of a wet, sloppy, dog kiss.

Graham shrugged. "Well, that's that."

"What do you mean?"

"I mean that's that. Horse love. It's a match. They've picked each other. Let's go wait by the practice arena."

Caroline scrambled to catch up. "Aren't we staying here to help? I'm not leaving her alone with that horse."

"She's not alone. Miguel's got this. You want something to drink? Water? Soda?"

"Graham, stop. I can't do this."

He took his time walking back as if he didn't know what to do. "What's wrong?"

She didn't bother to open her mouth because she didn't know what to say. It was irrational fear, confusion about Graham, and a complete lack of understanding of the horse world. Why had she come here?

Graham hooked a thumb in his jeans. "OK. Let me give it a shot. You're a mother. That kid is everything to you. Large horse, tiny girl, all this is new to you."

She nodded.

"Ava's not joining the marines, Caroline. She's riding a horse. They're going to brush Tilly, pick her feet, spray her down, and saddle her up. Miguel's going to find Ava the right size helmet and he's not going to let go this first time. They're going to walk around in a circle. You're going to watch and be proud."

She nodded again and dipped her head to hide the embarrassing tear that clung to her left lower eyelash. "You're right." She slashed it away. "I know I look like a crazy person.

THE FATHER-DAUGHTER PICNIC

Between my reaction to that super scary golf cart and that Trojan horse in there..."

He laughed. "Nah... You're not even in the top five of the crazy people I've met this week. You're a mom, that's all." He turned. "Can we go to the arena now?"

"Yes."

The scent of him brushed her nose as he walked away. More confusion rattled her brain. She wanted to cling to his side like Ava did.

This time it was her that reached for him.

She pulled back before he ever knew.

GRAHAM SAT THE NERVOUS mother on the wooden bleacher and put an icy can of diet cola in her hand. Shade from the spreading oak helped ease the burn of the late afternoon sun, but didn't help the typical Texas humidity.

He settled in nearby and downed a bottle of water. He was in over his head and it was his dad's fault.

I need you to take Ava and her mother to the barn.

It was easy for the old man to sit there and bark orders. Not so easy for them to gracefully decline. He took a long look at the beautiful woman on the edge of her seat. They'd both been caught between a crackpot old rancher and an excited six-year-old—and perhaps Graham was more caught than she was.

He'd assumed Caroline was single since he'd seen her on that unpleasant-looking date with that loser. But he hadn't known until yesterday that popcorn-loving Ava from the bank was hers, and he didn't know Caroline's husband was dead. It was that meddling Tammy Patty he'd grown up with in church who'd filled in the details whether he wanted to hear them or not.

He didn't like knowing personal things she hadn't told him herself. They already had a strained connection. He liked the kid, was attracted to Caroline, and admitted he enjoyed the pretend family dynamic they had for five minutes in the barn. But he was a short-timer in Cardinal Point and good, respectable men didn't mess with single mothers when they had nothing to offer them.

Then again...

He liked the woman in spite of their total distaste for each other. That's the reason he'd tried to comfort her when she was clearly freaking out about Tilly. By pure accident, what he said seemed to help. She'd lost so much, and everything that was new and looked dangerous was a threat of more loss. He understood that.

She tapped a nervous staccato rhythm on the side of the can. "Where are they?"

"They'll come out over there," Graham said and pointed. "I'm sure Miguel's giving her a basic safety lesson. She'll be fine."

She nodded and pulled the long mass of dark hair off her neck. She whipped it into a mound of some kind at the back of her head and secured it with a small, smooth stick she'd found on the ground.

Graham tried not to find that sexy or adorable.

"It's hot out here," she said.

"Yeah. A lot of work here in the spring and summer takes place early in the morning and in the evenings." He opened another bottle of water. "Any questions?"

"Yes." She didn't take her eyes off the ring. "Why does your dad keep telling everyone the Feds are coming to get you?"

He shouldn't have had the bottle of water at his mouth at the time of the question. Sheer will kept him from doing a world class spit-take as he fought to keep the water in his mouth and not choke to death.

A hint of a smile teased her lips. "Nice save."

"Thanks." He tossed the empty bottle toward a nearby barrel. "I guess my dad thinks he's funny, or maybe he's confused, but the Feds are not coming for me. If they wanted me, I'd already be in jail."

"But you are in trouble."

"No. More like a...situation."

She leaned back and rested her elbows on the seat behind her. "Explain."

Explain? Since when was she interested in anything about him?

She turned her pretty, dark gaze on him. "Seriously, tell me," she said as sweet as honeysuckle on the back porch vine. "Is it bad? Are you OK?"

Except for his lawyers and his dad, he hadn't talked to anyone about his trouble. That, he realized, was a sad comment on his lack of friends and a social life.

"I didn't do it." He slid his boot along the seat below him and tapped at the dirt that fell off the sides. "There was a major cyber security breach where I work. Accounts, money, people, records. All things I was in charge of were compromised."

"I see. That can be cleared up, right? There are ways to track these things and find the source."

"Yes, but this isn't like the guy down the hall hacked my password and logged in under my name. It's global. Whoever did it was at it a long time. Through password changes, firewalls, whatever security we had in place. They knew it all. By the time the damage was detected, it looked like it was happening through my computer while I sat at my desk."

"Does anyone think you actually did it?"

"I don't know for sure, but I don't think so. I haven't gained from it. There's no evidence I stole and sold identities or moved money around. There's no connection to me at all except for my name, my computer, my files, my access..."

"And you're thinking they have to pin it on someone."

"Don't they? I'm the scapegoat. I don't even think it's one person. It's a sophisticated phantom program somewhere overseas that set me up."

"Someone set it in motion. Could it be personal? Or someone inside?"

"Not inside. Had to be random. Out to get the company, maybe. Out to get me? Probably not."

"They'll figure it out, Graham. They're experts in the field."

Empathy radiated from her genuine hopeful smile. She did everything but hug him and tell him it'd be OK. He wasn't about to look more pathetic and admit the rest. He was the guy in charge at the time. He'd lose his job when they cleared him because someone had to. Then no one would hire him because no one would ever trust him again. Yeah. Her hopeful thoughts were exactly hopeless. His career would not survive the mess.

So again, he had nothing to offer them.

THE FATHER-DAUGHTER PICNIC

That didn't stop him from trying to change the subject by treading into dangerous water.

"Now can I ask you something?"

She fanned her face with her hand. "Why not?"

"That Davey guy in the restaurant the other night. Is that a thing?"

"It's less than a thing. It's a non-thing."

Abject terror knotted his intestines when he realized he had no follow-up. *Stupid, stupid, stupid.* The natural next move would be to ask her out and he'd already decided he couldn't do that. So what should he say? *Gee, I'm so glad you're not serious about that total moron?*

That shy smile teased her lips again. She apparently loved it when he was being the dumbest man on the face of the earth.

"I have to tell you something," he said. "I know about your husband. Tammy told me."

She sat up and reached for her soda. "I'm not surprised Tammy's been talking. She means well. It's not a secret."

"It's your personal business. You're new around here. You should share things when you're ready."

"Well, between Tammy and Bette, I'm sure there's nothing left to share."

"I'm sorry that happened to you and Ava."

"Thank you. Me too."

"Is Bette an aunt or something? She makes it quite clear she not Ava's grandma."

Caroline's wide smile erased the worried expression she'd worn since they got there. "No, she's a family friend. She and my mother were close. She's been with us since Jason died."

He nodded.

"I'm sorry again about Brent," she added. "I've been thinking about that since we've been here. It must be hard for you."

"Yeah, there's good and bad here. Someday I'm going to reconcile it all and it might be bearable."

"I know exactly what you mean." She turned his way after a long but easy silence. "Well, look at us. We're a couple of depressing blobs of humanity."

"No we're not," he said and jumped off the bleachers. "We're not."

She shook the can and then downed the last liquid that sloshed around the bottom. "You're right. We can't dwell there." She stood and tossed the empty can in the barrel. "There are plans. There's hope and a future."

"Exactly." He took her by the shoulders and turned her to face the edge of the ring. "And speaking of hope and a future, there's yours."

Caroline made a squeaky gasping noise and raced for the rail. She'd have flown right over if it'd been any lower. "Ava!" she yelled. "Over here!"

Ava smiled and waved and then returned her focus to Miguel.

Caroline yanked on the front of his shirt. "She's not looking at me, Graham. She stopped waving. She's scared."

He peeled her fingers from his T-shirt. "She's not scared. She's trying to listen to Miguel. Let her concentrate. He's got her holding the horn right now, but he'll let her take the reins in a bit to get the feel of it."

Caroline shielded her eyes from the sun. "That horse is so big."

"Tilly comes in at sixteen-two, so yes, she's large, but they both look completely calm."

"I can't believe Tilly doesn't belong to one experienced person. She's so beautiful."

Graham hesitated. "She did have a dedicated owner, but that owner doesn't come around anymore."

"Why?"

"Brent bought that horse."

"Tilly is Brent's horse?"

"No. Not his horse. He bought her for his girlfriend. He had a lot of people looking for that horse. I think Brent really loved that girl, but we sure didn't see much of her after he died."

Caroline rested her chin on the top rail and didn't say a word.

"I think that's why Tilly and Ava picked each other," he said. "Tilly's an orphan and Ava... Ava has..."

Caroline turned a wary eye on him. "Yes?"

"OK, I don't mean Ava's an orphan. What I mean is... You see, Caroline, horses are smart and sensitive and—"

"It's all right. I know what you mean." Tears puddled in her eyes. She turned away. "I should be filming this." She reached for her phone.

"No. Don't do that," he said. "You enjoy the moment. I'll get the video."

He adjusted his own phone to catch the event. He couldn't ditch his proud, stupid grin as the cooperative horse and its happy rider did their thing. The kid was a natural.

"They'll be around in a minute," he said. "I'll try to get some photos for Bette and my dad."

He glanced her way and expected to see her hooked on the fence, not missing one step.

Instead, she was watching him.

"What?" He pressed the stop button. "What's the matter?"

"I don't know what to do with you, Graham. I can handle your blustery old dad, but I didn't expect to have this kind of afternoon with you. You put me off guard and make me question some things."

"And that's bad?"

"I don't know."

"I appreciate the honesty," he said and repositioned his hat on his head. "So, I'll be honest with you."

"How so?"

"I know exactly what I should have done with you."

"What's that?"

"I should have kissed you that day in your office when you wanted me to."

Bachelor #3 - Condescending Connor and the Controversial Comment

Uccello Rosso.

Any other night, Caroline would be dreaming of a warm garlic knot as she read the swirling letters on the restaurant's glass double doors. *This* night, she hoped only for pleasant conversation and a quick exit—or anything in the world that resembled a sign she was doing the right thing for her and Ava. She no longer knew.

It seemed like such a logical plan when she set it in motion. Need a strong, loving father in the house so your daughter doesn't go looking for love in all the wrong places? Go online. Need a companion so you can make a baby brother and sit in church like a Norman Rockwell family? There's an app for that.

"Clearly, I am unwell," she muttered to herself as she swiped on a fresh coat of lip gloss and headed for the busy hostess stand. *Please, please, please, don't let Graham and his Chamber of Commerce cronies be here tonight...*

"Caroline?"

"Yes?"

"I thought that was you."

"Connor," she said and extended her hand. "Nice to meet you. I was about to ask for a table."

"I've got it," he said.

Caroline stepped aside and studied his gorgeous profile and exceptional clothes. She checked the recipe in her head. If you took any one of the James Bonds for style and charisma and added Bradley Cooper's hair and eyes, you got a Connor.

He turned her way and smiled. "It'll be a sec," he said, pressing closer because of the crowded space.

Oh, man, that cologne...

Yes, please.

Caroline moved to the edge of the small lobby and tried to control her school-girl stupidity. Yes, there was definite attraction. Who wouldn't be attracted to that? But was there chemistry? Was he a decent guy? Did he want to make a baby brother for Ava?

Her mind and body had apparently gone looking for forgotten territory. Attraction. Chemistry. *Babies?*

She'd smack her ovaries if she could reach them.

The hostess signaled for them, and Caroline tried to calm her raging... whatever was raging. Yes, she was young and healthy, but this was no time to lose focus.

Business. This was business. She had to vet these guys. If they got to the next round—and to the next—only then would she explore the other stuff. Like... was there enough there to keep a fire going?

Evidently, her hormones wanted to speed up the process. She'd noticed the other day that things had changed. Certain thoughts started to return. Her body was trying to discuss things with her they hadn't talked about in years.

"This is better," Connor said as he pulled out her chair. "We can talk now."

And they did.

THE FATHER-DAUGHTER PICNIC

All the small talk came up and was dismissed with an exchange of basic information and details. She showed a picture of Ava and Tilly, he shared a photo of his dog.

He nudged his water glass forward. "Who do you like for Cardinal Point city council in the May local election?"

This is where she would have pinched her thigh if she hadn't gotten over that habit. Politics? Really? He didn't even live in Cardinal Point. He lived in the next biggest city to the west. And didn't he know you had to ease into the heavy topics like religion, gun control, and who the next *Bachelorette* should be? They must've checked off similar boxes on the dating form or they wouldn't have landed in the same ball park, but she wasn't about to share her personal voting record with him.

"I don't know," she said and smiled. "I don't have all the facts yet."

Turns out, Connor had all kinds of facts. And opinions. Opinions he didn't mind sharing because, apparently, Connor's opinions were the right opinions, and everyone else's opinions were short-sighted and conceived from a lack of knowledge.

Connor, right. Everyone else, dumb.

At least that's the way the condescending jerk came off.

She attempted to steer the conversation somewhere else. "So, you're an attorney," she started. "Tax law? Family law?"

"Neither. I recently moved to a firm that specializes in medical law." He waved for the waiter to refill his tea glass. "I know you work in the field, so... full disclosure."

"Do you see yourself as more of a medical professional defender, or more a patient rights kind of guy?"

It could go either way. Both needed it. There was a lot of negligence across the medical field. But there were also patients who brought frivolous and unfounded complaints.

"I would say both. The firm's founder is Eli Mustin. He handles all the work for Dr. Sanders."

She stopped her napkin at her lips. He was naming names?

"That's not confidential," he rushed to add. "The legal team is constantly in the news."

Dr. Sanders... Dr. Sanders... Oh no. Dr. Sanders, the physician-assisted suicide doctor?

She pinched her thigh.

More than once.

"I can see by your face you recognize the name."

"I do," she said. "In my field there are many very sick and miserable patients. I've been asked..." She let the words drop off. She wasn't about to discuss this controversial issue with him. She didn't owe him that, and she didn't want to talk about it.

"C'mon, Caroline, your line of work is exactly why you should understand this." A caustic, condescending tone laced his words. "As a society, we don't even let a wounded dog lie there in pain without easing its suffer—"

"Stop talking." She snatched money out of the zipper pocket in her purse and put it on the table. "Thank you for coming and for sharing, but I have to go. It's not you, it's definitely me. OK, maybe it's a little you." She pushed in her chair. "None of this is working for me. I was wrong."

Her heels tapped faster and louder as she weaved through lasagna-filled tables. The exit was in sight. Clean escape. There would be no more of this.

THE FATHER-DAUGHTER PICNIC

She reached for the handle, but it moved in front of her. She sailed through. "Thank you," she said.

To Graham Hollister, who held the door.

CAROLINE PULLED INTO the safety of her garage and pushed the button. She plucked her phone off the floorboard where it'd slid as she left *Uccello Rosso*. There was a text from Graham.

Is everything all right? Ava OK?

"Yes, Graham," she said to the phone. "I'm fine. By the way, why do you always pop up like a painful, exploding pimple when I least want to see you?"

Yes. I was in a hurry. Thanks for asking.

The tap on the passenger side window caused her to jump and drop the phone again. "Geeze, Bette, you scared me. What are you doing out here?"

"I came to ask you the same thing. Are you planning to come in... or...?"

She retrieved the phone. "I'm coming. Is Ava in the tub?"

"Nah, she's already in bed."

Disappointment hit her like a truck. "Really? It's not that late." She shut the door and slung her purse over her shoulder. "I wanted to see her."

"Sorry, boo. She's still exhausted from all the ranch excitement night before last. All she wanted was to get in bed and look at the horse book she got from the school library today."

Caroline sagged against the car. "Horses again."

"Oh yeah," Bette said. "That's not going away." She shuffled toward the door in her bunny slippers. "Why are you home so early? Wait. Don't tell me. The mail-order groom you picked out brought the two sister wives to the rendezvous. Sorry, baby. Did you think you'd be the only one?"

"Not tonight, Bette." Her feet refused to take her weary body another inch.

Bette made a sharp turn and headed back. "Wait a minute. Did something happen?" She grabbed a garden tool and held it up. "Where did you leave him? I'll cut that internet predator."

"That's a rake, Bette."

"I'll rake that internet predator."

The garage door opener light clicked off.

"Don't move," Caroline said. She used her phone screen to make her way to the switch on the wall. "Put down your weapon. It's not him, it's me. I'm a horrible mother."

Bette dropped the rake where she stood and cinched her robe. "Not this again."

"It's true. I work too long and don't spend enough time with Ava. My body has started some tribal mating dance behind my back and, yes, it's time to admit my plan to find a father for Ava may not have been my brightest idea. Worst of all, I have to tell my hopeful six-year-old that Tilly is never going to be her forever horse. I should've never taken her to that ranch."

"All right." Bette pushed her into the house. "Let's stick a pin in that tribal mating thing for a minute. We're definitely coming back to that. Right now, I'm going to make tea and we'll discuss the other stuff."

THE FATHER-DAUGHTER PICNIC

Caroline dropped into a kitchen chair. "I don't want tea. There's nothing to discuss. You were right. I tried to force something that cannot be forced, and I opened myself up to situations that were more stressful than helpful. And I don't need more stress."

"Can't say I'm sorry that's over, but I am sorry you had a bad experience."

"I pinched my thigh again."

"You should put ice on that to ease the bruise." The kettle whistled and Bette poured a cup. "I saw Tammy today. She volun-told me I would be manning the sno-cone booth at the father-daughter picnic in a couple weeks."

"That's nice of you. I saw the park where it's held. It's on the same road out of town as the Hollister's ranch."

"Yeah, she said Whit would be there with all his girls and Ava, and she didn't want to be all up in his father-daughter business. More like father-daughter picnic equals Tammy's home alone. Can't blame her."

"I see the logic," Caroline agreed.

Bette came to the table with her tea and a package of chocolate donuts. "As for the horse business, didn't it turn out to be a positive experience for Ava?"

"Yes. You saw the pictures. It was perfect."

"The problem is...?"

"It's expensive. Coop Hollister waves his hand and makes things happen and gets a little girl's hopes up. I don't know if I can stretch my budget to handle boarding, feed, lessons, tack... Not to mention I know nothing about it."

"Welllll," Bette sing-songed as she waved a donut around. "Graham Hollister seems to be the best choice to help you out there."

Caroline didn't flinch, twitch, or blink. Any hint of interest, or any confirmation she'd had a good time with him at the ranch would be an invitation for Bette to lose her mind. "Yes, he was very helpful yesterday. As for tonight," Caroline hurried on, "did you have plans?"

"Oh no, I'm in for the night. I'm gonna continue to make sweet love to this package of donuts and watch *The Thorn Birds* on the classic movie channel."

"I'll check on Ava," she said and stood. "If she's really out, I may run back to the office if you don't mind."

"No problem. I should be alone with this chocolate, anyway. But you better freeze right there, sister. What's all this about a tribal mating dance?"

"Oh." She slumped back in the chair. "It's my hormones, Bette. I'm all tweaked up. It was a bad date, but I saw that gorgeous man and my mind wandered to some places I hadn't been in a while. I wanted things. I miss things... I didn't think I'd ever miss those things again."

"That is nature, honey. Don't beat yourself up about it. It was bound to happen. You're a young woman. You want things. It's OK."

"I know. It's one of the reasons I realized my stupid plan was so... well, stupid. I thought I was detached. I'm not. It's weird." She stood with her purse and stepped toward Ava's room for a peek. "I won't be long."

"Sure thing, and just an observation here, but..." Bette paused to lick chocolate off her hand. "I think it's interesting

THE FATHER-DAUGHTER PICNIC

you've had this change of heart about your plan and that all this *reawakening*, so to speak, has happened after you spent some time with Graham at the barn."

Don't flinch, don't twitch, don't blink...

Plastic crinkled as Bette stood and headed for her room. She caught Caroline's gaze and raised a perfectly waxed brow. "I bet Graham can help you with all that too. Don't you think?"

CAROLINE PARKED UNDER the portico and used her door card to enter the back entrance and head straight to Coop's wing.

She found him in his room, bathed in light from a small reading lamp hooked on his bed. He turned the page of his book as his readers slipped down his nose. No sweats, no pajamas, no robe. At eight o'clock at night, the man wore a white, button-down dress shirt.

She stepped inside and nudged the chair to the side of the bed. "You headed out to a party?"

"Nope," he said and closed his book. "They have me practicing with my buttons and zippers and belts."

She smiled. "I see."

"It felt so good to be in my own clothes, I didn't take 'em off." He lifted the blanket to reveal a pair of gray dress slacks.

"Are you going to sleep like that?"

"I might."

He looked good. Better than good. Color had returned to his cheeks and his eyes had brightened and smoothed his usually sour face. He'd turned the corner on therapy, and if he wasn't in a rehab center, it'd look like he was relaxing in his office at the bank. Except for one tiny red nick by his sideburn, it appeared he'd re-mastered a shave. Somehow, he'd managed to trim the ear hairs that troubled Ava so much.

"You're on track to be released soon. You've met most of your goals. The social worker should be talking to you as early as next week to start getting things set up to go home."

"Well, a bet's a bet." He paused and then met her gaze. "You didn't come for our game yesterday, and you're here late today. I hope it wasn't because my fool son did something to upset you at the barn."

Hmmm... Upset her? No. Irritate her? Yes. Like a mosquito buzzing her ear, his assumption she wanted him to kiss her that day, well, it was his arrogance at its best.

"No. It was a nice visit. And you need to stop telling people the Feds are coming to get him. That's not going to happen."

"You seem sure."

"And you're not? Your son isn't a criminal."

He shrugged and put his book on the bedside table in exchange for his phone. "Graham said he sent pictures and a movie, but I can't see them."

"Let me try," she said. "If I can't find them, I'll send them to you from my phone."

"So little Ava had fun?"

"The best time. You have a beautiful home. That barn is a kid's paradise."

Coop tucked his glasses in his pocket and held his arms across his chest. A faraway glint in his eye said he'd hit on a memory. His thin lips pursed and then curled at the corners.

THE FATHER-DAUGHTER PICNIC

"My boys used to watch old westerns on Saturday afternoons," he said. "Then Sunday after chores and church, they'd spend the rest of the day out riding and reenacting what they saw. Lunch was at our place. The Hunts and some others always came... The boys, they made a day of it. Their mothers had to drag them in at dark and..."

He stopped there as if the rest was lost. Or maybe he'd let it go on purpose.

"That's a wonderful memory," she said. "Your sons had an awesome childhood on that ranch."

The amusement that had played in the crinkles around his eyes faded. "Maybe," he said. "Seems like a hundred years ago." He shifted in the bed and moved his weaker arm into a different position. "What about you? Any childhood vacations to the Grand Canyon you want to share? I got all night."

"No." She sighed. "No Grand Canyon. We weren't really a vacation kind of family."

His expectant gaze invited her to go on, but he didn't ask. Salt-and-pepper eyebrows, raised in anticipation, and the fatherly look in his crisp blue eyes compelled her to continue with a story she hadn't ever shared.

"We tried to take a trip from Texas to Florida once. I was about five-years-old and so carsick in the back of my dad's Ford. My mom and dad fought a lot. In Mississippi, I picked out a candy bar at a convenience store. It had a bug in it."

Coop put a hand to his ear. "You said *a bug*?"

"Yes, I opened the wrapper and there was a dead bug stuck in the chocolate. My dad was like *sorry, baby, we'll get another one somewhere else,* but my mom said *give me that, I want my money back.* So we turned around and they kept fighting. My mom got sick in the motel that night. She stayed in bed for two days."

"In a Mississippi motel?"

"Yes. The third morning she stuck me in the car and we left. She said we were going back to Texas."

"Without your dad?"

"Yes."

"Was your mother still sick?"

"She didn't seem to be, but she did that a lot as I grew up. She'd say she felt bad and spend a few days in bed, but there never seemed to be an explanation. Then she'd snap out of it."

"How long did it take your dad to get home?"

"A long time. Weeks." Her chest hurt at the thought of the long-buried memory. "I thought he was stuck in Mississippi and couldn't get back. You can't imagine the nightmares and the panic... Anyway, I realized much later he'd made his way to Texas, he just didn't come home. My mother said he didn't want to because of me and because he didn't want to be bothered by us."

"But that wasn't true."

"No. My mother was mentally ill, Mr. Hollister. I didn't understand it for years. We saw my dad less and less. He couldn't take it, or maybe he didn't know what to do, but I see now he tried. He was in way over his head."

Coop scrubbed a hand across his face and then worried the edge of the blanket with his shaking fingers. "I know one thing, Caroline. Your father loved you very much."

"I always believed that," she said. "But I don't understand why he left me there. I was a baby wildebeest alone with a lion. A psychotic lion. Why didn't he come get me?"

THE FATHER-DAUGHTER PICNIC

"Men don't like to look their failure in the eye, and they do an even poorer job of handling guilt."

"You think he considered me his failure?"

"No. You were the light of his life. But you were the reminder of every failed attempt to help your mother with her illness. He loved you, Caroline, and he wanted you, but he didn't know what to do with you."

The hint of tears glittered in his eyes. They'd waded into some deep, murky water and she didn't know whether to let him sink or go for help.

She leaned in. "We're talking about Brent now, aren't we? About how you tried to help him?"

"Maybe," he whispered so softly she almost didn't hear. "Or maybe it's about the things I did that didn't help at all. The things that made it worse."

"You loved your son, Mr. Hollister, and if I've learned one thing about mental illness, it's that it's a hard war to fight. Winning is only as possible as the patient's willingness and ability to participate in their care." She touched his arm. "Sometimes everything you have isn't enough."

He turned his attention from the edge of the blanket to a piece of thread that dangled from a buttonhole on his shirt. He ripped it free. "I thought you were looking for my pictures."

She smiled. "I am. Your phone is seriously in need of a routine update," she said and searched the screen. "I think that and the lack of signal in here kept them from loading. I'll keep trying but, in the meantime, look at mine."

A sparkling smile returned to his face as he swiped his way through the images. "That's Tilly. How did they meet?"

"To hear Graham tell it, it was fate. They chose each other."

"Looks like a match to me." He started the video. "Yep. Look how comfortable they are with each other. You have a natural horsewoman there."

"That's what I've heard."

"Did you get everything set up with Miguel? When does she go back for her next lesson?"

"I need to talk to you about that. I appreciate that you wanted Ava to see the horses after she talked your ear off about how much she loves them, but I'm not in a position to buy a horse and all the trimmings, and I don't think my six-year-old can get an after school job to pay her way."

"Who said anything about all that? Everything she needs is at the barn."

Yes, he would say that. He hadn't seen Ava looking at the riding pants and boots Bette pulled up for her on the tablet.

"I'm sure Miguel's time is not free, Mr. Hollister, and Tilly is a valuable horse."

"All right, enough of this. You and money can't stand between a girl and her horse."

"Spoken like a man who doesn't worry about money or the proper sized helmet for a first-grader's still-thickening cranium."

He waved her words away with her phone and pointed toward the bottom drawer of his bedside table. "New, wrapped deck of cards in there," he said. "We'll play for the horse. One hand. If you win, Tilly belongs to Ava."

"You can't be serious."

"As a heart attack. I wouldn't be snappin' your garters over something as important as a horse." He tossed her phone aside and prepared to lower his bed stand to use as a playing surface.

THE FATHER-DAUGHTER PICNIC

"Think of how much fun it'll be someday when she tells her friends her mother won her first horse in a poker game."

"Or, how much *not* fun it will be when she tells her therapist how her mother *lost* her first horse in a poker game."

"You haven't lost to me once. Why start tonight?"

She'd be suspect of an intent to lose on purpose, but he was nothing if not a worthy competitor, and he had all the appearance of a man with integrity.

"We can work something else out, Mr. Hollister."

"Why would we? One game. Winner owns the horse."

"You already own the horse."

"Not if you win the hand."

"You need to rest." She stood and grabbed her purse and cell. Ava's lit-up face filled the phone screen as Tilly's white-gold mane flicked in the breeze on what had turned out to be one of her daughter's happiest days.

She dropped her bag. "One hand. Winner gets the horse."

Candidate #3 - The Hometown Heroine

Graham hit the door at Songbird's as J.R. Hunt got out of his car nearby.

"Hey, Graham."

"Mornin'."

"Breakfast meeting?"

Graham held the door. "No. It's blueberry muffin day. Thought I'd take some to the bank. What are you doing here? Home from Austin for a long weekend?"

"I came home so I could have that talk with my dad last night."

"Oh. How'd it go?"

J.R. adjusted the bill on his UT baseball cap. "He disowned me a couple times. Disinherited me once. My mom took me back on his behalf."

"Is it all smoothed over this morning?"

"Yeah. Stacey and I have enlisted the help of an expert to draft a proposal. It's happening. I'm going to graduate in May, propose to my girl, and then we're gonna be the happy but poor developers of a non-profit. As you can imagine, my dad is beside himself with pride."

Graham laughed. "He'll come around. And congratulations on the engagement."

The moment seemed to call for one of those half man-hug-chest-bump things. He'd watched this guy grow up with Brent. J.R. had an education, a plan, and the woman of his dreams. And last night he'd stood up to his overbearing father.

Graham had somehow been a part of that. He embraced his friend and suddenly felt older than his years.

And very much alone.

J.R. took another step in line toward the counter. "How's your dad? And how are things at the bank? Have you found your replacement?"

"Dad's made great progress. Could be home as early as next week."

"Wow."

"As for my replacement, do you remember the Flores family from school? Julie would have been way ahead of you, but you probably knew her sisters. She's coming in this morning. She did college and training through the military. Looks promising on paper."

"I remember that family. All those girls went through ROTC." J.R. nodded toward the counter. "You're up, buddy. And, hey, thanks for everything. Watch your e-mail. It's not the official proposal, but there's something I want you to see."

Graham nodded. "Will do."

The small, older man behind the counter held up a box. "What'll it be?"

"I need a dozen blueberry muffins." He paused. "Make it two. Cash the Armadillo might be hungry."

GRAHAM TEXTED CAROLINE while he waited for his nine o'clock candidate.

Congratulations. I understand you now own a horse. Miguel has the paperwork. You can get it tomorrow when you take Ava to the barn.

Umm... there's paperwork?

Graham smiled. *I'm afraid so.*

He paused and considered his next move. Just tapping out the words made his heart pump faster. *Would you like to go for a ride with me tomorrow while Ava has her lesson?*

Golf cart or horse?

You know I mean horse.

Suddenly, the three floating dots on the screen meant everything. Yes? No? The suspense made his right eyelid twitch in time with his thumping heart.

OK. As long as the horse is old and slow, preferably with asthma or COPD so it won't want to get excited or run...

He laugh-snorted like a teenaged girl and was immediately grateful he was alone in his office.

Done. See you tomorrow.

The tap on his door left no time to contemplate the ride.

He stood to greet Julie Flores. He recognized her now, that brilliant yearbook-picture smile still the same. All the Flores sisters had served or currently served their country, and their photos appeared in the local newspaper on a regular basis. They were soldiers and heroines and had worked all over the world. So why did the talented Julie Flores take an interview to work in the hometown bank?

"Julie, come in."

"Graham, it's been too long. How's your dad?"

"Surprisingly well considering how bad he hurt himself and how much he annoys his care team."

"Glad to hear it," she said and found her seat. "I think we're too young to tell each other we haven't changed a bit, right? Because it'd be a tragedy if we actually had at this point."

"I think that's right," he agreed and opened her file on his desktop. "This is impressive, Julie. Tell me more."

Julie Flores was everything the bank needed. She knew the community, the culture, and the job. She knew his father and half the board, and her diplomatic skills and experience were worth the largest salary he could offer.

If his job took him back tomorrow, he could leave and not look back. His dad's return was iffy, at best. Even if he physically healed and could prove his mental capacity to do the job, did he want to? Would the board let him?

"Julie, based on your credentials and this interview, I'd gladly recommend you to the board as my first choice but, I have to ask you, why Cardinal Point? You could work anywhere and make a lot more money. You could open your own consulting or accounting firm. I mean, literally, you can do anything you want to do. Why here?"

Her expression was as certain as any he'd ever seen. "I've seen the world. I've served my country, and I've gotten an education. I'm engaged. My fiancé's tour will be over soon. He's not from here, but he doesn't want to go back to where he lived." She leaned forward. "I do, Graham. My parents are here. I want to raise a family here."

He envied the resolve in her eyes. The purpose. The sense of belonging. His only thought had been how fast he could get back to his career in Houston. Even with Caroline and

Ava tugging at his heartstrings, he knew they were better off without him. Cardinal Point reminded him of nothing but failure. He didn't need to let them down too.

He nodded. "I understand."

"I'll do a good job for you and your dad. I look forward to hearing from you." She stood and picked up her bag. "Thank you, Graham. All I've ever wanted to do is come home."

Bachelor #4 - Online Dating Status Change: Account Deactivated

Ava darted out of Caroline's reach and sprinted to Miguel's side. She and Tilly greeted each other like old friends, and Caroline's list of warnings and instructions faded on her lips. Her daughter turned with a smile, and all Caroline could manage was a tight little wave and a *be careful* that was lost in her daughter's bubbling laughter.

She stood in the middle of the barn alone, except for the startling sneeze from a horse to her left named WonTon. The earthy scent of manure and hay met her nose in the humid air as she stepped closer. "I know how you feel, buddy," she told the horse before she walked on. "Spring allergies are the worst around here."

She didn't spot Graham until she exited the far end of the barn. He had two horses saddled and tied to a post in the shade of a massive oak. He sat under the tree in the same worn jeans and boots from the other day. She stepped back inside before he saw her. Like a little boy, he picked up a twig and scratched at the dirt before he snapped it and found another. And like a little girl, she clung to the edge of the doorway to spy on him.

"Wow... Focus," she whispered to herself. "I need clarity. I need to determine if there anything real here for me and Graham."

The question had kept her up half the night. The boy under the tree was not the arrogant jerk she'd made him out to be. If anything, he was unsure and alone, and didn't seem to belong with his dad in a place where he'd spent his whole life. And what did she know? She was the plotter of the ridiculous dating plan and a woman whose hormones were conspiring against her. She and Graham could really need each other, or she could be the victim of her own lonely sorrow. Was it real, or was it the puddle of grief they waded around in together that drew them to reach for each other?

Graham stood to check his phone as she left the barn and headed his way.

"Hi," he said and hurried to put away his cell and dust his hands.

"Hey." She motioned to her jeans and old cross trainers. "I don't have riding clothes, but I know by the online tutorials I watched that women usually don't ride in off-white capri pants and wedges."

He dipped his head and smiled. "You look great."

That look and comment kicked a dent in her resolve to not be moved by his charm and good looks.

Fail.

He took the bridles from where they rested on the saddles, and slipped one on each horse. "You've met Marigold, she's your ride for the day. Small, slow, and knows these trails. This," he said and motioned to the larger horse, "is Jasper."

"The famous Jasper." She petted the paint horse's neck like Ava had done. She gazed up into his large and beautiful but mischievous eyes. "You're a handsome boy, but you sure didn't do Coop any favors, did you?"

THE FATHER-DAUGHTER PICNIC

"He's young and ornery, but he's learning. C'mon." He pointed to the stirrup. "Get on up on Marigold and sit for a minute until you're comfortable. I've got something for you."

"I think I've got this." She positioned her left foot and grabbed the saddle. "If I can't pull myself up and swing my leg over this little horse, you should send me home and never speak to me again because I'm hopeless."

"Not a chance," he said and laughed.

In one fluid movement, she made it. She didn't know what to do next, but she was up there.

"Take the reins. Hold on to the horn if you need to." He took the rope from the post. "This is the lead rope. We'll wrap it here. That way I can grab it in a hurry if Marigold goes nuts and runs off or something."

"Is that possible?"

"No." He pulled a piece of paper from his pocket.

"What's this?"

"Tilly's bill of sale."

She unfolded it. "That's absurd. I didn't buy her."

"No, but she's yours. The old man wanted it official."

"This says I won her in a poker game."

"Didn't you?"

"Yes, but how is this official? I haven't told Ava, by the way. I need to work out with your dad and Miguel how to pay for all the other stuff."

"You'll figure it out. Maybe you need to play more cards with him."

"I'm not doing that." She held the reins as well as her breath. "What do I do with these?" Everything she'd read and watched online escaped her head in an instant.

"Don't worry about it right now. We'll practice. She knows the trail and she'll follow Jasper. If you want to stop, pull them back with a *whoa* and she'll stop. She'll wonder what all the fuss is about, but she'll stop."

Caroline shrugged. "There's that, I guess…"

Graham mounted Jasper. Strong, confident, and so… *manly*. She was transported back to the western romance novels Bette hid under her bed that summer she stayed with them. She'd sneaked into the pages and wondered what the big deal was—until she read about what happened under the stars with real cowboys and the women they rescued from runaway wagons on the prairie.

He pulled beside her in total control of the gorgeous but high-spirited horse. "Ready?"

Oh my…

"Yes."

"We're gonna head out that way and to the back of the property. There's a creek if we make it back that far. I've got some water. Need anything else?"

What she needed was to take him apart and find the ticking center of him.

She needed to make an attempt, bare her own soul, and jab at some buttons to see if anything was real.

"Yes," she said. "I need you to take me to the old barn."

GRAHAM HEADED LEFT around the pond. The old barn would come into view, just after the stand of oaks, and beyond the dilapidated stretch of fence that held his mother's forgotten

THE FATHER-DAUGHTER PICNIC 109

blackberry bushes. He'd been there a few times since Brent died, but it'd been a while.

Marigold dutifully kept the pace behind him. He'd hoped this would be a good day for him and Caroline. Time to talk. Time for fun. They'd laughed—a lot—when they stopped so he could teach her how to use the reins, but now quiet had come as they approached the barn.

Bird songs and insect noises penetrated the steamy air as bright morning sun heated his skin. Uncertainty turned in his stomach and wrestled with enough fear to make him feel like his insides could collapse and kill him at any time.

But he wasn't afraid of the barn.

And he wasn't afraid of the grief.

No. He was afraid of her.

He led them to a shady spot and hopped off to tie Japer to the same hitching rail he'd used as a kid.

Caroline glanced at the ground on either side of the horse as he came to her side.

"Come down the same way you went up."

She nodded, and it was clear she already knew. She'd found the natural rhythm of the animal and would be a competent rider in no time. Wherever these Bishop women came from, there were cowgirls in their bloodline somewhere.

Still, he put his hands at her waist as she dropped. The urge to press his fingers into her sides as she slid down his body was too much. She tried to tug away at first, and then relaxed.

Stray hairs from her ponytail teased his nose as he bent to her ear. "Why did you want to come here, Caroline? And don't say it's because you wanted to see an old barn."

Her body stiffened against him as she placed her hands over his.

He squeezed harder.

"I'm not trying to hurt you," she said on a fading breath. "I'm trying to know you."

He let go as if he'd been singed. "I'll get the bridles off and get us some water."

She gave Marigold a scratch and mumbled something to her, but mostly she stayed close to him, watching him work the tack, and tie the quick-release knots on the rail. Her presence made his breath shallow. What did she want from him, and why did she want it? He already knew he didn't have enough for her. The thought of the three of them living some idyllic life on the ranch appealed to him, but it's not what he was allowed to have. He wasn't worthy of her.

In his world, he failed people. He couldn't risk failing her.

"It's beautiful here," she said. "So nostalgic. Right down to the sprinkle of bluebonnets. It's like a picture from one of those magazines about Texas scenic highways and wildlife." She motioned to fresh tracks. "Looks like people have been here."

"It's not off-limits. Dad's hands store things here, and any boarders who ride these trails can come through here."

She nodded and took the water he offered. "Are those yours?"

"What?"

"Those birds. That pair of cardinals has been chatting up a storm since we got here. I think they're working on a nest in that clump of yaupon."

He twisted to see where she pointed. "They're wild birds. How could they be mi— Wait a minute. Don't tell me you've

THE FATHER-DAUGHTER PICNIC

been soakin' up the crazy about all these cardinals flying around. News flash. They're not specific to Cardinal Point, and they don't all represent dead people. Sometimes a cardinal is just a cardinal."

"Except when it's not."

"You're friends with Tammy, right? She got you going on all that? You know the Chamber of Commerce started inviting that baby of hers to ribbon cuttings. Like a baby can handle those giant fake scissors."

"Hey," she said and laughed. "That *Royal Redbird Baby* thing is a big deal."

"I guess." He caught a glimpse of the birds. He wasn't going to tell her the same pair had been nesting there for at least three years. He knew that because the female had a damaged right eye. She'd shown it to him one stressful morning when he'd run to the barn with a bad idea.

Caroline moved closer to the trees, trying to get a better look.

He wiped the trail of sweat from the side of his face. "I didn't mean to imply that everyone who has a belief like that is wrong or weird or whatever."

"It's fine." She smiled. "Just because you don't believe something doesn't mean it isn't true."

He stood and put his empty water bottle in his pack. "OK, I can see I'm out of my spiritual league here, so I'll shut up."

"No, don't you dare shut up. Talk to me."

He waved his hands in frustration. "I don't see the point. If a higher power or the universe wants to show me something, it can be in anything. The horse, that stump, the Word. It doesn't have to be some mystical appearance of a bird everyone talks about. Can't it be specific to me so I don't mess up and miss it?"

"Sure." She walked toward him. "I agree. I always thought if God wanted to talk to me, he'd talk, and I'd understand it was him talking, no matter how the message came through. But I can see how the bird thing is comforting."

She picked at the wrapper on the water bottle and didn't look at him.

"You had a bird encounter, didn't you?"

"If you must know..." She kept her gaze glued to the bottle. "I did."

He leaned against the rail. Legs extended, arms crossed, he settled in. "Tell me. I won't say anything."

She sidled up beside him. The scent of vanilla and raspberries wafted between them. Marigold nosed at her for attention. Caroline reached out to stroke her as if she were an extra-large dog.

"When we first came here, the realtor was driving us around to look at houses to rent. I picked up flyers everywhere. I read the story of the cardinal on one of them. I'd heard it before. I'd seen a poem about it. Anyway, at the third house, me and Ava opened the back door and a perfect male cardinal flew up and landed on the fence. Looked me right in the eye and did that thing where they tilt their head like they're really looking at you. Then he flew onto a chair on the patio as if he lived there. Like it was his home. And I felt it. I felt like it was Jason was telling me that was the place, that I'd be OK there."

Her chest heaved and then stopped. She made a tiny squeak and he knew she was trying to hold it all in and not cry. He put his arm around her because he was gettin' a little teary himself. He expected her to buck and brush him away. But she curled into his embrace like a warm puppy and planted herself firmly against him.

Perfection—but he had no idea what to say.

"It's not the bird, you know," she whispered. "It's the certainty the bird brings." She looked up at him and pressed her hand against his heart. "That kind of clarity is a miracle."

Clarity, miracle, blah, blah, blah... All he saw were lips, lips, lips.

Jasper snorted and nudged his head between them. Caroline laughed and wiped wet horse nose from her cheek. Graham growled. If there was ever a time to punch a horse...

Worst. Wingman. Ever.

Caroline wandered toward the barn door.

"No treats," he snapped at the horse. "No treats for you ever again."

She pressed against the worn, wooden panel. "Are we going in?"

"Yeah, we can go in." He moved the latch. "Let me go first, though. There could be any kind of animal in there. Watch for snakes. And there's lots of old equipment. And those hairy spiders you talked about."

She reached for his hand. "I'm not worried."

The heavy door gave way to the musty, thick scent of old wood and hay. The creak of the hinges and the flap of bird wings outside the high, closed windows reminded him of the owls he and Brent once watched from a spot in the loft.

She squeezed his hand. It took everything to peel away from her grip.

"I'll push open the other door," he said. "More light will come in."

"It's exactly what I imagined but it is dark."

"There's water and electricity, but it's not on. When everything is open it's bright enough."

The old tractor sat in a rusted heap in the corner. Go Kart and mountain bike remains lined a side wall. A stack of tires, an assortment of ladders, a pile of wooden crates. Everything from his childhood lived in this place, and he was still so...*numb*. Would any of the good feelings ever come back?

Caroline found a bunch of old window frames against a support beam. "Where are these from?" She tipped one forward.

"Not sure. Maybe an old house that was on the property."

"These are all the rage in country décor right now."

"I wouldn't know. They look like old windows to me."

Her smile balanced his teetering thoughts, but did nothing to ease his guilt or allow any peace to slip back into his soul. Numb was good while it lasted, but up this close to the place where Brent died, numb had to step aside and bow to the powerful shame that haunted him.

He'd missed the signs, lost the connection, and failed to hear his brother's cries for help. And she could ask about windows, and want to know him, and let him hug her, but she couldn't possibly understand the depths of his regret or the anger toward the lousy father who disregarded his every concern. There was no hope to amend his dysfunctional relationship with his dad, and there was nothing fair about letting her and Ava into it.

No. Hope.

She was at his side again, taking his hand, and working her fingers between his. "Are you OK in here?"

No. Hope.

Her soft words and inviting—no *begging*—gaze forced him to consider it.

No. Hope.

He opened his mouth. "I don't really know what happened in here. I mean, I know Brent died here, but I don't know specifically...*where*. My dad wouldn't tell me. I got here as fast as I could but the scene was clear by then. I was hours away."

She nodded. "Your father was protecting you."

"The very first thing I thought when I heard the news was that I was so glad my mother was already gone. It would have ruined her, and I doubt their marriage would have weathered the storm."

Thoughts came faster now. "There was no note, so the police had to take a look at everything. It's not a crime to kill yourself, but when it happens, especially without a note, they have to be sure it wasn't a homicide. The evidence overwhelmingly ruled that out. It didn't give us any closure, but one of the two things I learned from the only support group meeting I went to is that it's not uncommon. Especially in a violent death."

"What was the other thing you learned?"

"That the words *committed suicide* are no longer politically correct."

"I did not know that."

"It's because the word *committed* sounds like a crime and is upsetting to some survivors. We're supposed to say *died by suicide* or even *suicided*, but I can count on one hand the times it's come up in conversation, so I haven't used any of that."

"Was your brother in treatment?"

"No. Clearly, he should have been, but Coop Hollister had a hard time admitting there was an emotional problem. Thought he needed more focus and discipline and less coddling. I wasn't aware of how much worse he got after I left for college and went to Houston to work. I wasn't there for him."

"I'd say it's not your fault, but I think you know that."

"And I'd say I should know that, but I don't. And I'd say it's my father I blame most."

"And I'd have to say you couldn't possibly blame your father more than he blames himself."

He tore his hand away from hers and left the barn.

"Graham, what's the matter?"

He could hear her behind him as he stomped away, coming too close so she could drive him nuts. He turned on her. "Whose side are you on? I thought you wanted to know me, but I forgot you're Coop's number one fan because you two are all cozy with the cards and the late-night conversations." Yeah, he knew he sounded like an idiot, but that didn't stop him. "What are we doing here, Caroline? Don't play games with me. My brain can't handle coming up with strategy right now."

"I am on your side. I do want to know you. But I also know all this anger you carry around toward your dad is not punishing him. It's punishing you. Your dad and I do talk, and I can tell you, he takes all the blame for Brent. Someday you're going to have to air this out with him. He almost died in

THE FATHER-DAUGHTER PICNIC

that accident. Do you really want another death in your family without closure?"

Frustration jetted through his veins at warp speed. "What would you know about it, Caroline? Huh? What experience do...?"

Well, that was it. He was officially the biggest jerk in all the land.

Tears hit her cheeks faster than she could hide them. Rage brought visible heat to her face and dried them before she had to.

"Do you think this is easy for me? Do you think I want to see you in pain? Or relive my own?"

"I'm sorry, Caro—"

"You've not cornered the market on grief. You don't get to do this alone anymore. We have more in common than not. I'm hurting, you're hurting, your dad is hurting, Ava is hurting... I'm tired of all the agony I heap on myself. Aren't you? I know the grief will not go away. I know I will never *get over it* as well-meaning people like to say. And I don't even think it has to get better. But I do think it has to get *different* in a way that we can move on. We have to manage the anger and the bitterness. We have to let in some light."

Everything she said made sense and he needed to hear it. The only problem was, the pain and anger was chunked so deep in his soul he couldn't find it to start chipping it loose to let it go.

She rubbed her temples and squeezed the sides of her head like she had a migraine. "Do you know why I'm here, Graham? Why I'm really here?"

"No," he mumbled, though it was clear she wasn't waiting for a response.

"I'm here because for, whatever reason, I like to be with you, and that scares me. I have a child to think about, and I want her to have what I didn't have. I was raised by an unmedicated bi-polar mother and an absent father. Yeah. I know about that stuff too. I'm a cornucopia of dysfunction." She paced a line on the dusty ground in front of him. "I'm here because I'm tired of being sad and scared and in control of everything for every second of every day." She stopped, so close he felt her heat on his skin. "And I'm here because you are the only man I've wanted to touch me since my husband died."

He couldn't pull her into his arms fast enough.

Feather-soft lips met his in an eager embrace as the depth of her raw declaration settled in his brain. He deepened the kiss, and the next and the next...

Her arms tightened around his neck as they both fought to breathe.

"I think about you... about this all the time," he whispered into her hair. "But I have failed at everything, Caroline. I failed at being a son, I failed at being a brother. I've even failed at my job. I cannot fail you."

"Stop." She stepped back. "Don't say that. Clean slate. You've never failed me, you've never failed Ava, you've never failed us."

The boulder in the pit of him started to crack.

The only thing left to do was hold on to her.

And kiss her again.

THE FATHER-DAUGHTER PICNIC

CAROLINE STARTED LAUGHING and couldn't stop. She clung to the side of Marigold with one foot in the stirrup and both hands in position on the saddle. "I can't do it," she told Graham as she sagged against the patient, stinky animal.

She'd tried three times to pull herself up. Each was more of a comical fail than the last. Between the emotional blitzkrieg and the humidity, she neared total exhaustion. Truth be told, all the kissing had made her lightheaded.

And she was probably dehydrated since they'd run out of water.

The laughing only made it worse and zapped more of her strength.

Oh, and the passion-fueled high she was on from all the kissing...

"I need some help here, Graham. My booty is not one of my smaller... um... *ass*ets," she said with a snort. "I can't get it up there."

Graham came around to give her a boost. It's like he knew better than to laugh at her and chose not to laugh with her. He opted for a mischievous grin. "Your booty is perfect."

That wasn't true, but everything between them had shifted, and the place where they landed turned out to be something near perfect. Finally, things made sense and she had something to feel positive about. Finally, there was laughter.

Judging by Graham's demeanor and the way he kept looking at her, he felt better too.

"We're not late, are we?"

"Nah, we're fine. If Ava's not on the horse, Miguel will have her cleaning the slime out of water buckets. There's always work at a barn. She'll learn."

"Oh." She considered how badly she already needed a shower. "What do I have to do to help you when we get back?"

The flirty gaze he shot her made it very clear where his man-brain went.

"Don't look at me like that," she warned. "We're nowhere near there."

"I wasn't thinking anything," he clearly lied. "I was thinking I have a rake and a wheelbarrow with your name on it back at Marigold's stall."

OK, sure...

A streak of black and tan caught her eye at the far fence line. "Is that your dog?"

"No. That mutt belongs to the neighbors back in the woods. He's basically harmless, but he likes to run around over here and annoy the livestock."

Graham picked up the pace as they neared the barn. "I think they're still in the practice arena. We can ride over there first and you can show Ava how you're doing."

There was joy in his suggestion and joy in her heart when she heard it. The only embarrassing part was that her six-year-old was exuding confidence and natural ability on a giant show horse while she was trying to master basic moves on a retired and possibly wheezing petting zoo mare.

She waved like an obsessed fan when she spotted her daughter. "Ava! Over here!"

Ava smiled with her whole body. "Hey, Mama!"

THE FATHER-DAUGHTER PICNIC 121

Tilly stopped at the opposite side as Miguel spoke to Ava from his perch on the rail.

The black and tan streak from the field reappeared in the distance. He picked up speed and seemed to be coming straight for them.

"Graham, is that dog running this way?"

"Yeah, it's fine. Stay here. He likes to run up on the horses but they're used to it."

Graham nudged Jasper into a trot and headed around the outside of the circle.

He might be used to it, Tilly might be used to it, but Caroline wasn't. Isn't this the way horses spooked?

Graham's shout was lost in her ears as the dog barreled under the fence and straight at Tilly's back legs.

He barked. Tilly kicked. Ava wobbled and fell to the ground.

Caroline screamed but didn't hear it. She took off running on watery legs with no recollection of getting off her horse. "Ava!"

Graham got to her baby first, but she hit the dirt and pushed him out of the way.

"Ava! Are you OK?"

Ava tried to get up. "I'm OK."

Caroline stopped her. "Don't move. We need to be sure you're not hurt."

"I'm not." She scrambled to her feet.

Caroline caught her breath and rested on her knees when she realized...

No one else looked alarmed. Miguel hadn't even made it all the way around the horse to check on her. And Tilly? She was gazing down at Ava as if to ask why she was on the ground.

Graham sat on his haunches close by, looking like he was bracing for the punch.

"Are you people kidding me right now? She fell off the horse!"

"Caroline," Graham said and touched her arm. "Calm down."

A crimson haze of anger clouded her vision. "Surely, you did not tell me to calm down."

Ava twirled. "I'm fine, Mama, see?"

She stood and nearly knocked him off balance in the process. "You said she was safe here. You said you wouldn't let anything happen to her."

"Look, Caroline, she's fine. This happened exactly the way it was supposed to. I told you that dog annoys these horses. Tilly saw him coming, she got defensive and protected her rider. One kick and that dog ran off yippin'. Believe me, if she wanted to, she'd could've taken his head off."

"That's supposed to make me feel better? I'm supposed to feel good about my daughter seeing that?"

"No, of course not, that's not going to happen. All I'm saying is that Tilly did a great job. Did you see what she did? She didn't even swish her backside when she tapped that dog. Ava only fell off because she's still learning. You should be feeding her baby carrots right now and thanking her for doing the right thing."

"You are not making this better."

THE FATHER-DAUGHTER PICNIC

"The point is, Ava's gonna fall off the horse. She could be a gold medal jumper and she'd still fall off once in a while. It happens."

"Well, it doesn't happen to us. C'mon, Ava, let's go."

"I'm not finished. I have to collect all the brushes and put them away."

"We're leaving."

Ava chose that moment to assert herself. "No, I don't wanna go." She stomped her foot like she had as a toddler in the grocery store.

"Now is not the time, Ava. We're going." She tore Tilly's bill of sale from her back pocket and tossed it at Graham. "Here. I don't want your horse."

Tears rolled from Ava's eyes like a rain-swollen creek in the spring. "Tilly!" She wailed like a wounded animal as Caroline dragged her away.

Fueled by fear and disappointed beyond comprehension, she picked up her sobbing daughter. Ava's helmet banged against her as she fought to keep her in her arms.

She no longer cried for Tilly. Instead, she screamed at the top of her hysterical lungs for Graham to rescue her.

And Graham looked like the horse had kicked him in the chest with both legs.

Candidate #4 - Interview cancelled. Position filled.

Graham parked at the rehab center and collected three folders from the passenger seat. He checked his phone. He only thought the most important call he'd ever get was the one he got yesterday from his attorney. Not true. The most important call he'd ever get was the one that hadn't come. The one where Caroline agreed to put Ava's falling incident behind them and pick up where they left off. The one where they smoothed things over.

He had nothing but a blank screen. Apparently, she needed more time.

Graham tapped on his father's door. Coop stood at the window, fully dressed in the jeans and T-shirt he'd brought him a week ago.

"Graham," he said and shuffled toward him with only the slightest help from the walker. "It's about time. No one's been by for days. I'm going nuts in here."

"Sorry about that, Dad, but it's been a hectic week." He held up the folders as he found a seat. "But I have all you need to know right here."

Coop maneuvered himself onto a chair. "What've you got? When am I getting out of here?"

"Tomorrow. Eleven o'clock discharge time." He scooted the first folder across the small table. "I've been setting up all your home healthcare. You have an in-home rehab sched—"

"Forget all that. What happened at the ranch?"

"What do you know about that?"

"What don't I know? It's my ranch."

"Then you know what happened."

Coop pulled his readers off the bedside table. "I'm asking you. Caroline hasn't been by. Everything all right?"

"The kid fell off the horse."

"She get hurt?"

"Not even a little bit."

Coop put a hand to his mouth and tapped a finger at his lips as he thought about it. "Uh-oh. Her mother's as high-strung as they come about that kid. Bet she's steamed."

"You could say that. She's disgusted with all of us."

"She'll come around. Everyone falls off the horse now and again." He laughed. "I did."

"Yeah, I wouldn't make the comparison if you get a chance to talk to her about it. You on a rowdy horse that ended with a stroke, a head injury, and months of hospitalization will not help our case."

"I see your point. Have you talked to her?"

"Not really." Fresh fear hit him hard. What if she didn't come around? She said he hadn't failed them, but the first thing she did when Ava fell was call him on his promise to keep her safe.

"Well, spit it out, boy. Either you talked to her or you didn't."

"I'm trying, Dad." Aggravation propelled him out of the chair and to the window. "I texted to make sure Ava was all right. She answered me, but she's been slow to respond to anything else I've asked. I thought I might try to catch her here when we're done here. Some things need to be discussed in person."

"I see," Coop said. "How long have you been in love with her?"

He turned so fast his shoes squeaked. "Love? We hardly know each other. We've spent some time together, but now..."

"Look, son. I can explain it to you but I can't understand it for you so listen carefully. It's clear there's something between you. I saw it a while ago. She's a fine woman. That's a beautiful family you have there so don't mess it up."

"They're not mine, Dad, and it's not that simple. I know you're not long on patience, but there's a child involved so I have to wait it out." He returned to the table. "Can we move on? I have other news."

Coop shrugged. "Fine."

"I heard from my lawyers yesterday. I've been cleared. They want me in Houston to discuss it further and negotiate my return to work."

Coop's eyes widened with what seemed to be genuine happiness. "What did they have to say for themselves?"

"I think they've known since the beginning I had nothing to do with it, but they had to follow procedure. Turns out that state-of-the-art cyber security is only as tight as the employees who work in the system. Against all warnings and training, it only takes one person to click on the wrong e-mail and expose the company to a cyber assault. That's what happened, and I wasn't even the one who clicked."

"So you're going back to Houston. You're going to leave me and the bank." Hurt and fear flashed in his eyes. "And you're going to leave Caroline and Ava."

They'd shared a lot of pain over years, but never had his dad looked so vulnerable and alone. Maybe Caroline was right. He had changed.

"No, Dad, I wouldn't leave you without taking care of everything. I told them you were going home and I needed to make sure all is set up at home with your caregivers. And who knows what their terms are for taking me back? Maybe they're unacceptable." He tore at the edges of a folder. "As for Caroline and Ava, they're not mine to leave."

"I didn't raise you to be a quitter."

"I'm not a quitter, but I can't make a woman talk to me. Do you think I'm not working on it? Do you think it's not the most important conversation of my life?"

Coop leaned forward and tapped the table. "What else?"

He pushed Julie's folder toward him. "We've made a decision on the bank manager."

"I plan to go back to work."

"That's fine. It's your bank. No one will say you can't work, but this is business. We're in expansion mode. Someone has to take the helm and put in the long hours. Someone who is mobile and energetic and up on all the latest technology."

"Someone who's forcing me into retirement."

"I'm sorry, Dad, but it's not like that, and you know it."

"You didn't hire the environmentalist, did you?"

"No. It's Julie Flores. I think you'll be impressed."

Coop thumbed through the pages. Deep frown lines creased his forehead as he scanned the documents. Graham knew his dad. He was searching for a reason to not like Julie Flores, and looking for ammunition to fight the decision.

Affection rose inside him for this difficult man who had raised him. Coop made mistakes, never admitted he was wrong, and never backed down either way.

He was a hard man, but he was still his father.

"What's this?"

Graham glanced at the page. "That's a list of current community projects we're involved in."

"And this?"

"That's a flyer for one of the events. We're a sponsor for the community-wide father-daughter picnic."

Coop set the flyer in the middle of the table. "It's this coming Saturday. I think we should go."

"Well, Dad, two things. We don't have to be there as bank reps. The marketing team is taking care of it. They'll be giving out bottled water with our name on it and bank koozies and balloons. And secondly, it's a father-daughter activity. Despite how you used to call me *Mary Margaret* when we put up hay, I am not a daughter."

"Let's make an appearance."

Graham held up his hands in surrender. "Sure. Why not?" It would do the guy good to ride around town and see what had changed in the time he'd been gone. He'd know people there and Graham could be a dutiful... daughter. "I'll get you settled at home tomorrow, then I'll drive to Houston for a day or so and see what they've got. I'll be back by Saturday to take you to the father-daughter picnic."

THE FATHER-DAUGHTER PICNIC

"Make sure you're in time to pick me up at twelve o'clock sharp."

Everything about that exchange sounded wrong. He didn't have time to dwell on it.

Coop rested his frail arm on Julie's resume. "What am I supposed to do with myself?"

Graham presented the last folder. "I'm glad you asked."

"What's this?"

"This is a project for which you are going to be an advisor and eventual board member."

"What is it?"

"It's a project J.R. Hunt is developing with his soon-to-be wife."

"The Hunt family is all hat and no cattle. What do they think they're developing?"

"Jim Hunt is your best friend."

"So?" Coop turned the page and stopped stone cold in the middle of a breath. "What's this about?"

"That is Hollister House. It's a mental health support center to be built in honor of Brent. It's a place for teens and young adults who are diagnosed with depression and other mental illnesses."

"What happened to Brent is our private family tragedy. It's not for broadcast on the side of a building."

"Tragedy yes, but our loss is far from private."

"How dare the Hunts dredge this up?"

"J.R. and Brent were close, you know that. And J.R. has other people in his life who struggle with bi-polar disorder. This is an effort to help as many people as possible so another family doesn't have to lose someone like we did."

"I don't like it." Muscles twitched in his father's face. His heart beat visibly beneath the thin skin on his neck.

Graham grew concerned for his health. He attempted to pull the paperwork away. "You don't have to look at this today."

"No." Coop's hand came to rest on his. Rough, but warm. Hard and still soft, his father squeezed. "Leave it."

Graham withered beneath the gentle touch because Coop didn't touch. He didn't hug, he didn't comfort, he didn't wipe away little boy tears. He'd never experienced the powerful heat in his dad's finger. He'd never seen his dad cry.

Until today.

Today, tears splashed on weathered cheeks and it was all Graham could do to stem his own.

"I'm not ashamed because Brent had a mental illness," Coop said. "I'm ashamed because I didn't do anything about it."

Graham paused in the unfamiliar intimacy of the lingering moment. "I understand, believe me, no one understands that better than I do."

"No." His hand slipped away. "Do not try to share my guilt with me. You're not allowed to have it. It's all mine."

Words connected in Graham's head, but none sounded like an adequate reply. "I don't think Brent wants you to carry that burden. I think he'd say it's time to let it go."

No response.

"And no one's going to think about who did or didn't do something when they see our name on that building. It can only be positive."

Coop rested the folder against his chest. "I have to think about all that."

"Take your time. Right now, you need to concentrate on going home and gaining strength."

Coop's intense sky-blue gaze met his across the table. "Why am I alive, Graham?"

"What?"

"I thought I was dead when I fell off that horse. I should have died."

"Don't say that, Dad."

"I'd like to know. Why am I here? My arm is useless. I can't work. You don't need me. No one needs me."

"You're here because you're strong and stubborn and, clearly, God didn't want you yet. As for people needing you, do I have to remind you most of your business ventures support a lot of people in this town? And J.R. Hunt will be lost without you on his development team."

Coop didn't look convinced.

"Ava needs you," he went on. "Yes, apart from her rolling off the horse and her mother hating us, that's a good thing you're doing for her. She belongs on Tilly."

"Reckon we'll ever get them back?"

"We're gonna try, aren't we?"

Graham checked the time. "I have to go. Someone's coming to put grab bars in your bathroom at home."

Coop answered with a disgusted grunt.

He paused at the door. "I do need you, Dad. We only have each other. I need you for Thanksgiving and Christmas and Easter Sunday. And, without you, who would escort me to the father-daughter picnic?"

"That's enough, Mary Margaret," he said and chuckled. "And Graham..."

"Yes?"
"I love you, son."
"I love you too, Dad."

CAROLINE WAITED IN her office until dusk before she went to visit Coop. State regulators and corporate snoops had kept her so busy she hadn't had time to process the weekend and iron it all out. Ava stayed in a perpetual pout and asked constantly about Graham and Tilly. Caroline wrestled with all of it rather than sleep. The answer was somewhere between how perfect she felt in Graham's arms and how scared she was when she picked Ava up off the ground.

But right this minute Coop Hollister was preparing to leave in the morning. And that made her sadder than she ever expected.

She stepped into his room. "Mr. Hollister?"

He set his files and book on the table and removed his glasses. "Well, I wondered if you were going to show your face around here."

"What's that supposed to mean?"

"I understand you had a first-class hissy fit at my ranch."

"Ava fell off the horse."

"Was she hurt?"

"No."

"Was she scared?"

"No."

"Did she want to get back on?"

"Yes."

He waved his good arm and tapped his toe like an angry parent. "Then what was the hissy fit about?"

This was his attempt to scold her. She kinda had it coming.

"All *right*," she snapped back. "I overreacted. I'm completely mortified at my behavior." She plopped into the chair across from him and rubbed her tired eyes. "I got scared. I stopped thinking. Ava won't speak to me." She dropped her head onto her arm on the table. "I know I owe Miguel and all the other people around an apology. I owe Tilly a bag of carrots, and Graham... We had such a good day and he's so patient with Ava and I really hurt his feelings."

"So... You care about my son?"

She raised her head. "Of course I do."

"Have you talked to him? He said you haven't returned his calls."

"Not yet. He's been busy with the social worker getting all your home care set up. I've had some work issues here. We've texted. He says we'll talk but we haven't yet."

Coop smacked the table. "That's another thing. You two need to toss those phones in a ditch and get down to business. Doesn't anyone have a real conversation anymore?"

"You mean like this pleasant one we're having right now? I'll call him when I leave here."

Coop shrugged and made snapping noises against the table with the edge of his book. "Yeah. If you can catch him. He has a board meeting tonight and then he's leaving for Houston."

"What? *When?*" Her breath couldn't have left her faster if he'd driven the old tractor into her chest. "Won't he be here to take you home tomorrow?"

"Maybe. Miguel might have to come and get me. His employers want him back to work there."

"Wait. The suspension is over? He's in the clear?"

"Yes. He wanted to tell you all about it but, like you said, you've been busy and haven't returned his calls."

"You've made your point. Thank you." A different kind of fear made its way through her racing mind. "Maybe... Maybe he doesn't want to talk to me anymore. He didn't text he was leaving." She peeked at the phone in her pants pocket. "He hasn't texted anything for hours."

"I'm sure he wants to talk to you," Coop said with a slight but reassuring smile. "His lawyers wanted him back to negotiate his return. Who knows? Maybe they won't reach a mutual agreement. You'll work it out."

She put both hands on the table and prepared to stand. "OK. I need to go make some calls, but I wanted to come by and wish you well as you prepare to leave. I've enjoyed our time together, and I appreciate everything you've done for Ava. I'm truly glad you're going home and are doing so well, but I'm going to miss you." She pushed back her chair.

"Wait a minute, missy. What's that boring speech about? You talk like we won't see each other again."

"Sorry, Mr. Hollister, I'm a bit stressed right now and I need to sort all this out."

"You keep your seat. I'll sort it for you. First of all, you're going to bring that baby back to the barn and give Tilly back to her. That kid's growing on me. We have a lot of rummy to play, and I have a lot of things to teach her about horses."

Caroline nodded toward his walker, his cane, and his wheelchair. "Can't say I find a lot of comfort in that."

THE FATHER-DAUGHTER PICNIC

"Aw, that's two different buckets of possums. She's six and made of rubber. I am not."

"Secondly?"

"Secondly, everything is going to work out. It's as simple as that."

Simple. When had she ever done simple?

"I hope you're right."

"I am."

"Thank you. I'm going to go now, but I'll see you soon, and if you need anything during this transition, please ask."

"OK, I need something." He handed her a piece of paper. "I would like to invite you and Ava to go with me to the father-daughter picnic on Saturday."

Balloons and picnic baskets outlined the flyer. Smiling cartoon people sat on quilted blankets with lemonade. "I heard about this. Ava is supposed to go with my friend Tammy's husband and their four girls." She paused to consider the smiley-faced ant parade along the bottom. "I'm not sure I understand, Mr. Hollister."

"Have you ever been to a father-daughter picnic?"

"No. As we've talked about, there wasn't much of this kind of stuff at my house."

"I thought so. I haven't been to one either. The bank co-sponsors it every year, but I don't have a daughter."

"I'm flattered you would ask us, but it's a small town. People might start gossiping that I'm some long-lost love child or something."

"I don't care what people think, Caroline, and you shouldn't either. And if I did have a daughter or granddaughter, I'd want them to be like you and Ava so it all evens out."

Childhood disappointments weighed on her mind like slabs of granite. Besides Bette, no older, wiser, parent-like person in her life had ever regarded her so highly. "That's so sweet."

"Don't go cryin' on me now. It's a picnic." He pulled a deck of cards from his drawer. "If I have to, I'll play you for it. Be prepared to lose and lose big. I have one comin' to me."

She wouldn't dare. Not because she might lose and have to go, but because she might win and miss the opportunity. "That won't be necessary. Are you sure you're up for a day out with the two of us?"

"Yes. You'll have to pick me up, though. I think Graham hid my keys."

"I hope so."

"Call that number on there for Songbird's and have them fix us up a basket. Have them add lemon bars."

"OK. Anything else?"

"Yes. Make sure you pick me up at eleven o'clock sharp."

Caroline slipped out of the room and fumbled for her phone. She pressed Graham's number and waited.

Straight to voicemail.

The Father-Daughter Picnic

Caroline turned her car full of people into the parking lot. Coop whacked the dashboard with his fist. "Stop!"

She panicked and hit the brakes because surely a screech like that meant she was about to flatten a small child and his puppy. "What?"

"You missed a spot."

"I can't park in a disabled spot. Oh wait. I forgot about your temporary hang tag. I'll go 'round again."

"Hurry," he said. "Go around again before someone gets it."

"Yes, sir, that's exactly what I just said."

She sneezed from the cloud of perfume that wafted her way every time Bette moved in the back seat.

The gardenia-scented flirt stuck her head into the front seat between them. "You know, Cooper, my car is a bit roomier than this one. I'd be happy to take you anywhere you need to go while you're getting back on your feet."

"Thank you. I'll keep that in mind."

"There's another blue sign, Mama."

"Thanks, baby. I'll grab it, but I have to back up. Bette, can you move your big Texas hair so I can see?"

Bette glared at her in the rearview mirror. "If you like this," she said and patted the frozen blonde mass on her head, "you'll love the glittery bow I'm gonna stick on the side."

"I honestly can't wait to see that."

"Hey, Mama?"

"Yes, Ava."

"I think I know why these blue parking spaces are on each end."

"Why is that?"

"I think it's like that other park where there are paths on both sides so the people in wheelchairs can get there easier."

"I think you're right."

Coop tried to turn her way. "Well, you're as smart as a hooty owl, aren't you?"

Ava giggled. "Hooty owl."

Caroline stopped the car. "Let me open Ava's door, then I'll get your stuff out of the trunk and help you. OK, Mr. Hollister?"

"Let me out too," Bette said. "I want to help."

Caroline rolled her eyes and made sure Bette saw her. *Stop it*, she mouthed.

Bette answered by racing to Coop's door.

Caroline retrieved a wheelchair and walker and a cane from the trunk, along with a blanket, sunscreen and a small cooler. Oh, and a lawn chair because she was sure Coop didn't need to try and sit on the ground. "What do you want to use first?"

"Give me my walker."

"Are you sure? We don't know how far we have to go?"

"I'm sure."

She loaded everything else into the wheelchair. "I'm bringing this in case you need it on the return trip."

"I won't," he said.

"I might," she mumbled. "You three are wearing me out."

THE FATHER-DAUGHTER PICNIC

Bette flashed her a grin. "What was that, sweetie?"

"Never mind."

Ava skipped ahead. "Can we look for Mr. Whit and my friends?"

"Yes, but let's get settled first."

"Find us a tree that's not too far from the path," Coop instructed.

Bette stuck by his side and took the slow walk with him while she brought up the rear with a loaded wheelchair and a broken heart. Graham hadn't called and it was clear from his short and sporadic texts that he didn't have much to say.

The path wound through the trees and into an open area.

Ava stood with her hands on her hips in a vacant space. "This OK?"

"Yes," Coop called out. "Perfect."

So this was a father-daughter picnic. Dads of all sizes in cargo shorts and sandals herded daughters of all ages in sundresses and predominately pink and purple shorts. Blankets dotted the woodsy area and laughter rose like happy bubbles across the crowd. Booths with everything from face-painting to cotton candy and silver paper tiaras created a barrier to contain them in this joyful place where fathers and daughters were loved and celebrated.

It was a place she'd never been.

Caroline hurried to spread the blanket while Bette grabbed the lawn chair and took the opportunity to move closer to her target.

"Here you go, Cooper," she said and eased him into his seat. "Let me put this walker out of your way."

Caroline stopped her before Bette could put her chest in his face while pretending to... Good Lord, she didn't even know what she pretended to do. The woman was simply trying to put her breasts near his eyes.

"Don't you have a sno-cone machine to operate somewhere?"

"I'm going. Save me a piece of fried chicken."

Caroline put a bottle of water in his hand. "That was quite a walk. You doing OK?"

"I am," he said.

"I'm sure they told you not to be surprised if you tire easily for a while."

"Yeah, they told me a lot of things."

"All right. I'm going to the Songbird's food truck to pick up our lunch. Keep an eye on Ava?"

"Certainly. Have you heard from my fool son?"

She knew the question would come up, but she didn't know it would knock her feet out from under her. She knelt on the blanket beside him. "No. Not much. I tried to call. It must have turned out well for him at work. I'm glad."

"I wouldn't worry. I haven't heard much from him either."

"I'm not worried... Maybe it's all it's ever going to be. I've mishandled and misread a lot of situations the last few months."

"Everything is going to work out."

"You keep saying that." An acorn sailed onto the blanket from Ava's attempts to catch and feed a squirrel. "I'll get our food. You make sure she doesn't actually catch one of those fluffy-tailed rats, OK?"

"OK."

THE FATHER-DAUGHTER PICNIC 141

The line at Songbird's truck stretched around two trees and a port-o-pottie, but it went fast. She picked up their box and passed Bette in the sno-cone booth.

"Fried chicken. Don't forget," Bette called out.

"Cherry sno-cone," she answered.

"Hey," Bette yelled louder. "Your boyfriend's here." She nodded to the stand of trees where they'd come in.

Graham!

Relief swept through her. At least she could tell him face-to-face how sorry she was for the scene with Ava.

He scanned the growing crowd. She hurried to their spot so she could put down the heavy box and wave, but he needn't have worried about finding them.

Because Ava spotted him first.

Like a shooting star in a butter-yellow sundress, she streaked across the grounds and into his arms. With him in the proper attire—khaki cargo shorts and flip-flops—they walked hand-in-hand toward them.

Right there was the father-daughter picnic. The one she always wanted for herself. The one she wanted for Ava.

And none of it was really theirs.

She stood before him, breathless. "Graham. Hi. I didn't know you were coming."

"And I didn't know *you* were coming." He surveyed the scene and glanced at Coop. "What's goin' on here, Dad?"

"We're at the father-daughter picnic."

"Yes, I know, but is everything all right? You told me to pick you up at noon and you weren't there. The nurse said you were here."

Caroline was dizzy with relief and happy to see him, but she did manage to put it together. "He told me to pick him up at eleven."

Coop tapped Ava on the arm. "And look at that, hooty owl. We're all here. Somebody might be as smart as you are."

Graham's gaze never left hers. "Sorry. I don't know if he's playing games or having a relapse."

"I'm completely fine," Coop chimed in. "Except that I'm hungry."

Graham took her hand. "I need to talk to you."

"And I need to talk to you, but you left town and didn't call me back."

"Sorry about that, but there are things that shouldn't be said over the phone or in a stupid text message."

"That's the smartest thing you've said all week, son."

"Thanks, Dad."

Ava took paper plates and napkins out of the box. "Mr. Graham, are you gonna eat chicken?"

"Yes, please."

"I'll help you in a minute, baby." Caroline squeezed his hand. "The job. What happened?"

"I'm unemployed."

"I thought they wanted you back."

"They did."

Coop waved a chicken leg in the air. "Hey, the bank is expanding. Julie probably has a job for you. You should call her. All these new branches you promised me aren't going to manage themselves."

THE FATHER-DAUGHTER PICNIC

"Thanks, Dad." He closed what was left of the space between them. "We need to move this conversation somewhere private."

She nodded. "Absolutely."

"We'll be right back," he said and pulled her away. "You two behave."

"Aw, go on. We're havin' lunch."

Caroline yanked him back. "No! Don't go that way. Bette's in the sno-cone booth."

He dragged her off the main path and into a clump of trees and bushes around a forgotten picnic table.

"I have to tell you something, Graham." She slid to a stop in the dusty dirt. "I'm sorry about what happened when Ava fell. I'm so embarrassed and I'm so sorry I hurt your feelings. I know you'll keep her safe. You're going to have to take care of the horse part of this relationship. I'm unfit."

He pulled her against him. His soft laughter rumbled in his chest as he stroked her hair. "You're not."

"I am. Tammy says she can't go to her girls' soccer games without causing a scene. She has to stay in her car with the windows rolled up. I'm afraid I'm that mom."

Graham laughed again and set her away from him. "It's fine. We'll take it one step at a time." He glanced at the ground and let go of her as if giving her a chance to run. "You heard me say I'm out of a job, right."

"Yes, what happened?"

"I was cleared, and I thought all I wanted was to hear that and get back to work. But that's not what I want. As soon as I drove out of town, I felt like I had on the wrong pair of shoes or something. Nothing fits if I don't see you every day. Nothing works in my life if you're not in it. Four hours away is four hours too far."

Peace surrounded and settled her, but all the excitement popping in her brain kept coherent sentences away. "I can work with that," she finally said. "But Ava... you know she loves you but we have to watch what we do and say for a while. It's an adjustment."

"Yes," he agreed and pulled her back to him. "Like, I could say I'm already in love with you, but you'd think that's insanely too soon."

"Probably. And I could say I have some feelings of my own, but I wouldn't want to rush anything."

She leaned in, sure he would kiss her, sure she'd have to tackle him if he didn't do it soon.

"I have one more confession."

"Now?"

"Yes. I want to clear something up."

"What?"

"Those are my birds."

It took her a second. "The cardinals? You lied to me?"

"I didn't lie. I will never lie to you, Caroline. I never said they weren't. I just never confirmed they were."

"You should be an attorney for the government."

"Do you want to hear this or not?"

"Yes."

"My mother had an eye injury right before she died. She had these long fingernails, and she'd get agitated... We think she poked herself. They put a bandage on it, but it never got better. After Brent died I was filled with rage, naturally. I got so mad one morning I went out there to burn down the barn so I didn't

THE FATHER-DAUGHTER PICNIC

have to look at it. I had everything I needed. And then that bird with the injured right eye landed on the rail. I've lived here all my life, so I knew. I knew my mother had come to stop me from doing something stupid and dangerous."

The intensity of it all caused her to sag against him. "That's it. That's the answer."

"What is?"

"Remember, I told you? It's clarity." She pressed her hand against his heart. "Clarity is a miracle."

"Nothing has ever been as clear to me as this is right now. You, me, Ava... That's all the clarity I need."

She waited for his kiss.

He didn't disappoint.

Thank you for visiting Cardinal Point!

Please leave a review, and check out our whole series.
(Sweet Romance unless noted.)
When Love Leads You Home (Inspirational Romance)
The Father-Daughter Picnic
A Promise for Tomorrow
My Half-Price Valentine
A Blessing of the Heart (Inspirational Romance)
Almost Home for the Holidays (Inspirational Romance)
The Widow's Christmas Ruse
It Happened One Winter
Love at The Bluebonnet Inn
Red, White, and Baby Blue
Love, Lattes, and Lonely Hearts
Dr. Noah and the Sugar Plum Fairy (Inspirational Romance)

About the Author

Carla Rossi has been writing sweet romance and inspirational romance since 2004. She is a multi-published, award-winning author as well as an editor, cancer survivor, lifelong musician, speaker, and writing teacher.

For clean YA supernatural fantasy, visit Carla's other pen name, **Carla Thorne**, for her Warrior Saints series.

Made in United States
Troutdale, OR
08/18/2024